the cat

the cat

edeet ravel

PENGUIN
an imprint of Penguin Canada

Published by the Penguin Group
Penguin Group (Canada), 90 Eglinton Avenue East, Suite 700,
Toronto, Ontario, Canada M4P 2Y3 (a division of Pearson Canada Inc.)

Penguin Group (USA) Inc., 375 Hudson Street, New York, New York 10014, U.S.A.
Penguin Books Ltd, 80 Strand, London WC2R 0RL, England
Penguin Ireland, 25 St Stephen's Green, Dublin 2, Ireland (a division of Penguin Books Ltd)
Penguin Group (Australia), 250 Camberwell Road, Camberwell, Victoria 3124, Australia
(a division of Pearson Australia Group Pty Ltd)
Penguin Books India Pvt Ltd, 11 Community Centre, Panchsheel Park,
New Delhi – 110 017, India
Penguin Group (NZ), 67 Apollo Drive, Rosedale, Auckland 0632, New Zealand
(a division of Pearson New Zealand Ltd)
Penguin Books (South Africa) (Pty) Ltd, 24 Sturdee Avenue, Rosebank,
Johannesburg 2196, South Africa

Penguin Books Ltd, Registered Offices: 80 Strand, London WC2R 0RL, England

First published 2012

1 2 3 4 5 6 7 8 9 10 (WEB)

Copyright © Edeet Ravel, 2012

ONTARIO ARTS COUNCIL
CONSEIL DES ARTS DE L'ONTARIO

Manufactured in Canada.

LIBRARY AND ARCHIVES CANADA CATALOGUING IN PUBLICATION

Ravel, Edeet, 1955–
The cat / Edeet Ravel.

ISBN 978-0-14-318352-5

I. Title.

PS8585.A8715C37 2012   C813'.54   C2012-904286-2

Visit the Penguin Canada website at **www.penguin.ca**

Special and corporate bulk purchase rates available; please see
www.penguin.ca/corporatesales or call 1-800-810-3104, ext. 2477.

ALWAYS LEARNING   **PEARSON**

for S R S

and for Stanley Quinn, in memory of Barbara

Her cage was in the upper corner of the room. There were three rows of cages, and many of the cats, when they saw us coming, jumped out of their tubs, stretched their paws through the diamonds formed by the criss-crossed wires, and meowed at us.

I remember how drawn my son was to those cats, the ones who wailed for our love. He asked me to open several cages, and he held the friendly cats in his arms, stroked them when they leapt to the floor. One was a charcoal and pearl-grey tabby, a second was black with a regal white crown and white polydactyl feet, a third was tiger-gold.

But I had already decided on the cat we would take home. The cat I wanted didn't move from her tub when I peered into her cage. She only looked at me with deep, intelligent eyes. Even when I unfastened the cage door, she didn't leave the small plastic basin that was now her bed. She had given up hope.

I lifted her gently and set her down next to the tub. A sudden clanging in the next cage startled her, and I stroked her, murmuring, 'It's okay, kitty, it's only the noisy door.' She began to purr immediately. I'd never heard such a loud cat purr. When I lifted her in my arms, she trembled, but the purring didn't cease.

My son wished he could take all the cats home. It made him sad that we could adopt only one and had to leave the rest behind. I promised him the others would soon find homes. I pointed out that some of the identifying cards on the cages were already marked 'Held.'

I showed him the cat I had chosen and he stroked her with his small, six-year-old hands. We laughed at her incongruous purr. When he touched her cheek, she licked his fingers, and his face lit up in a mosaic of delight.

I told the people in charge that she was the cat we wanted. They were pleased we'd chosen her. She'd been at the shelter for six weeks.

It may have been because she was timid that no one had wanted her, but I thought it more likely that her appearance was the deterrent—she was ratty-looking, her fur the clashing colours of a tortoiseshell, and there were pale yellow blotches on her muzzle that could be taken, at first glance, for a runny nose. And yet the shelter had been optimistic. They must have been counting on her gentle personality to win someone over.

We filled in forms, answered questions. The shelter did not allow same-day adoptions, and we were given an appointment for the following day. My son was very impatient. We wished we could explain to our new cat that we would return, that we had not turned our backs on her.

On the way home my son said he would call her Amelia, after the pilot, because her purr was as loud, he said, as an airplane motor.

But the next day, as we drove back to the shelter, he said Flora was easier to say in a cuddly way. That evening, as our cat cautiously surveyed the borders of my son's bedroom, he decided that Flora wasn't right either. He mulled over names throughout supper, and we considered a long list of possibilities, but the following morning, as the cat lay purring on his chest, he exclaimed, 'Persephone!' We knew at once that we'd landed on the perfect name, and we hooted with triumph. Persephone, or maybe Prrsephone. Pursie for short.

Pursie, little Pursie.

And now because of Pursie I am forced to stay alive.

september

At least I have no close neighbours.

That was the idea, when we moved here, my son and I. Or rather, that was my idea. For my son the attraction was fields and trees. A four-room cottage surrounded by wild grass, and beyond the grass, forest.

And at the same time, a ten-minute bike ride from town. This was the wonder, I told my son, of small towns. You can live in the country and the city at the same time.

Now both the house and the town fill me with terror.

It's not what I would have expected—this feeling of panic. You'd think that once the worst has happened, there would be nothing to fear. But fear has gripped me and it won't let go.

What frightens me is this alien planet. A planet without my son. I don't know this world, I don't understand it, I've never been here or even heard of it. How can I negotiate this unknown place? How can I help but be terrified?

Pursie is not afraid. She knows something is wrong, and nuzzles up against me, hoping to console and be consoled. She searches the house for my son. She burrows under his navy fleece-lined windbreaker.

⸺◈⸺

Only sleep relieves me of fear. At midnight I take a small chalk-blue pill, and since my body isn't used to drugs, I drift off almost immediately. At my feet I feel the deliberate rhythm of Pursie cleaning herself. How can she be so single-minded in this shiftless place?

My sleep is deep and dreamless. Or rather, I don't remember my dreams. When I wake, it is as if I had swallowed the chalk-blue pill only minutes before, and the morning light surprises me. My pillow is wet with the tears I shed during the night.

The first thing I do each morning is reach out for the amber-tinted bottle of pills on my nightstand. I hold it in my hand and stare at it with hatred. The tint prevents me from seeing the chalk-blue pills inside the bottle, and this adds to my resentment. I should resent Pursie, not the potion that binds to a GABA receptor, but I direct my anger at the opaque container, with its white childproof cap. I want to pour these pills down my throat and die. Instead, I must haul myself out of bed and open a can of cat food.

My son loved Pursie.

⸺◈⸺

Pursie was two years old when we adopted her.

Now she is seven and my son will be eleven and eight months forever, though his child's bones will age. My son.

My old self would have considered it ironic that my son was killed by a child psychiatrist. The child psychiatrist fell asleep at the wheel of his car and swerved off the road. My son was crouching in the wild grass in front of the house, studying a spider, or maybe coaxing a ladybug onto his hand. It was Saturday morning, a few minutes past ten. The psychiatrist was coming home from his AA meeting, though he was addicted not to alcohol but to drugs he'd prescribed for himself.

But he wasn't on anything when his car ran into my son. Or so the local paper reported. He was only tired.

If the psychiatrist had fallen asleep a few seconds earlier, a few seconds later. If I had called my son in for a snack. If I'd been there to pull him to safety.

But there are no rewrites in life. No matter how implausible and unlikely an event, there is no rewriting it.

Did he suffer? I was told that death was instantaneous— a rib pierced his heart. The doctors assured me that the blow to his head had rendered him unconscious, and he did not suffer. But is there such a thing as instantaneous death? The body needs time to close down. What did my son experience as he lost consciousness? Did it take one second, two, five?

When I heard the screeching of brakes and something else, something horrible, I ran outside, but at the same time it seemed to me that I didn't move at once, that I was slow to react. My legs were heavy, as if determined not to rush, because after all, nothing had happened, it was probably nothing, there was no need really to get up and check, though I might as well.

I came out of the house and saw a burgundy car on the front lawn, and my son on the ground, and a tall, balding man bent over him, one hand on his cellphone, the other checking for a pulse. I didn't associate the car on the grass with the fact that my son was lying on the grass, curled up on his side but with his legs strangely twisted behind him. I assumed he was ill, and a passerby who happened to be a doctor had stopped to help. A Good Samaritan, I thought.

I tried to speak but a foreign language came out of my mouth. It was as if I were speaking in tongues—my brain sent words to my mouth, but only garbled sounds came out.

And then there was an ambulance and police cars, and my life as I knew it was over.

When I came home, thankful for the hospital sedative that had given me back the power of speech and enabled me to invent a friend who was meeting me at my house, the first thing I did was dial the number of the phone company.

I knew that if you refused to answer the recorded voice, if you said nothing, eventually a human would come on the line. I remembered the discussion we'd had, my son and I, about the strain of speaking to a machine. 'It's because you have to convince yourself that you're not a robot too,' my son said. 'Just put on a robot voice,' he advised, and demonstrated.

Now when the condescending electronic voice greeted me, I wanted to smash the computer that generated it, but the drug distanced me from my own rage, and I waited in a stupor until at last a man's voice replaced the recording. I instructed him to disconnect my service. Gearing up to dissuade me with special offers, he asked, in his heavy accent, 'May I ask why?'

I felt as if someone had struck me. In my addled state, it seemed to me that I was being mocked by a malevolent kōan, and I wanted to hang up, but I was afraid the line would not be disconnected unless I answered. 'Madam?' the man prodded. A still-functioning part of me told him that I was leaving the country, and he wished me bon voyage. 'Yes,' I said, and hung up.

I went out to the shed and fetched a saw from my toolbox. My plan was to release carbon monoxide from the furnace pipes. It seemed simple and logical—there was a limit, surely, to what anyone could be expected to endure. Even if there was nothing after death, I wanted to join my son in that nothingness. I wanted to be with him.

And then Pursie woke up from her nap and meowed. I'd forgotten all about her. She came up to me and purred her airplane-motor purr.

I stared at her with horror. Instantly I understood my predicament. I broke into a wail that sent her dashing. For a few moments help had been at hand, and I had reached out for it, but it had slipped away. I wailed for my dead son, and for what lay ahead.

———

I was suddenly colder than I'd ever been in my life, and I felt sick to my stomach. Spasmodic shudders, similar to the reflex that sometimes jolted me pleasantly as I fell asleep, ran through me, but these shudders came in quick succession, and were as powerful as waves crashing on rocks.

I lay down on the sofa and covered myself with my son's navy windbreaker.

The sedative rocked me as if I were on a raft, and quelled the shivering, but the nausea remained. I welcomed the nausea. I welcomed physical suffering of any kind and would have thrown myself against the wall had the drug not weakened my will.

I sat up, fumbled for a sheet of paper and wrote in handwriting I barely recognized:

> Dear Neil, our son was hit by a car and
> died instantly, or so I am told. I hope
> it was instant. He's at the hospital, you
> can look after things there. He wouldn't
> have wanted a funeral and if you
> arrange one I won't be part of it. But
> you will do what you want. Of course
> you still have Sherry and her children.

It was a cruel, unfair letter. I knew that Neil's love for our son was as boundless as mine. But everything was simple now—now that nothing mattered. There were no longer any rules, there was no need for pretence.

I climbed on my bike and though my body was limp and numb and I thought I might vomit at any minute, I headed for Neil's house. I took the two-lane highway that runs along the outskirts of the town. I rode on the unpaved shoulder, unable to remember or understand the farmland and woods, the half-finished construction on recently ravaged lots. Twice I fell.

Only as I neared the turn-off did familiarity return. I recognized the flat-roofed industrial buildings, the shabby shopping centre. I was aware that it was a beautiful day, sunny but mild, the air faintly carrying a sweet autumn smell. School would have started in a week.

I turned at the intersection, rode past lone garages and a nameless nature reserve, and made a left on Cityview Drive—more of an afterthought than a street, and perfect for Neil, with long stretches of vacant or forgotten land, a haphazard array of dissimilar houses, and the Toronto–London railway slicing it in two.

I made my way to the copse facing Neil's clapboard house and hid behind a cluster of trees. It occurred to me that for the first time in my life I hadn't thought about my stain. For the first time in my life I wasn't hiding because of it. I was hiding to make sure that everyone in Neil's household was indoors.

I stared at the house, at the cluttered front porch, the asymmetrical windows. The junk on the porch was indefinable, useless, waiting to be discarded. Garbage limbo: Sherry's trademark.

Neil's black Mazda was parked in the driveway, but I didn't see the van he'd given Sherry anywhere on the road.

I felt like the Angel of Death. I imagined a giant shadow creeping over the house, enveloping it.

I dropped my bike to the ground. With unsteady hands I collected wildflowers and leafy twigs. Cradling them in the fold of my shirt I crossed the street. As I stumbled through the obstacle course on the porch, metal edges scratched my ankles and, when I knelt down, my arms.

I arranged my miniature pyre on the straw mat and laid my note on the summit, anchoring it with twigs so it wouldn't blow away. Then I rang the doorbell and rushed back to my hiding place.

I stood, as still and frozen as a block of ice, behind the trees, my heart racing. The door opened, and Sherry's daughter looked out. How old was she now—fourteen? Fifteen? She'll be glad, I thought. It's Amy's lucky day, I thought.

Maybe it's misleading to say that I thought this or that. I wasn't thinking anything—I was merely aware of words flashing in my mind like banners in the sky. I was aware also of my repulsion, of my desire to throttle Amy, but at the same time I was removed from those feelings.

She sniffed the air distastefully, frowned, and was about to retreat inside when she noticed the note. She picked it up, read it, and turned abruptly back into the house, slamming the door behind her.

It was then that fear took hold of me. Terror such as I'd never known before seized my body and held on like the tentacles of a monster plant.

I mounted my bike and cycled back to my house. If I were falling through outer space I could not have been more afraid.

———◦———

I came home drained. My son was gone, my extraordinary, beautiful son. It was all I could do to walk to the sink, cup my hand under the faucet and bring the tepid water to my parched mouth.

I collapsed on the sofa. I wanted to lie on my son's bed, crawl under his blankets, but I didn't dare enter his room. I had to keep his small realm untouched, I couldn't let a single crease or dust mote shift or go astray. His things were all I had left. His things were rare artefacts, the last remnants of civilization, the key to everything. I barely allowed myself to breathe when I passed the doorway to his room.

I covered my eyes with my arm. As the drug wore off, hallucinatory nightmares took over. I was neither awake nor asleep but traversing instead some circle of hell in between. Pursie was dead on the floor, she'd been tortured and mutilated, and then another cat, and another— thousands of cats. And not only cats. The room was filled with the mutilated corpses of cows, horses, frogs—of hundreds of animal species in fact, and I couldn't step over or past them, nor did I want to. I knew that if I could bring them to life, my son would come to life too, but I didn't know the secret code, the secret incantation that would resurrect them. I could only gaze, horrified, at their bloated bodies.

And then my son appeared—he was fine after all, it had been nothing but a false alarm, a mistake. But when I tried to touch him, he turned into a cat and dashed out into the street and a car ran over him—a station wagon— and I was the driver of the station wagon. And the words of a country song, *sweet Jesus ... sweet Jesus ...*, distorted and jangled, were blaring on the radio, even though the radio was switched off, and this terrified me even more. I tried to smash the radio with a flashlight, but I couldn't silence it. The scratchy, distorted song continued to blast out of the dead radio.

The nightmare seemed to go on for hours but it was still mid-afternoon when the doorbell woke me.

I didn't move. I realized I hadn't locked the door and I heard the hinges creak slightly, and a woman's hesitant voice saying, 'Hello? Hello? Elise? May I come in?'

———

She could not have been kinder, gentler, more tactful. She was from the Bereavement Centre, she said, and she wanted to help in any way she could. She wanted to see if I was all right. She'd brought tea and homemade cookies.

I let her in. I didn't want to talk to anyone, see anyone, but at least she'd released me from my mad, misfiring brain.

She was a lovely woman. Her soft brown hair, her compassionate eyes, her athletic body, taut with a desire to comfort—I could not find any fault with her.

And yet whatever tatters remained of my being, I felt them swelling with resentment. How dare she enter my house, how dare she address me? The chasm between us reflected my despair back to me. But I said nothing.

She put on the kettle, found cups and plates, brought
the cookies to the coffee table. She gave me two books
and some printouts in a folder, and told me about the
Bereavement Centre. I wanted to hurl those books to the
floor, rip them to shreds. Books! What role could they
possibly play in my life? What could they possibly tell
me? I did not want to be consoled because I could not be
consoled. To suggest that consolation was possible—by
way of books, of all things—was to advertise the wild
inability of this woman or anyone else to understand
what had happened. It sealed my isolation.

She sat next to me on the sofa. Even her dress, an ill-
fitting navy blue shift, was tactful, as if she knew that the
merest ornament would be an affront.

'What a friendly cat,' she said, as Pursie jumped up
clumsily to the sofa. My son and I used to laugh at her
clumsiness, at the hit-or-miss thumps, the noisy flurry
of her efforts to transport herself from one surface to
another. 'What's his name?'

'Pursie. My son named her,' I said, gasping for air.
Uncontrollable weeping shook me without mercy. I
wanted to stop, I wanted not to cry, but my brain refused
to obey me.

The bereavement woman put her arm around me,
handed me tissues. She'd come prepared.

'We have one-on-one counselling,' she said. 'We want
you to know we're here for you.'

Like all clichés, the words were a lie. No one was there

for me. No one was there, period. The world had emptied out. My son was the last, the only, gift, and now he had been taken away.

And his gifts—my son would never receive the endless gifts that had awaited him. The millions upon millions of treats and presents I had planned and anticipated for him. A lifetime of presents.

It was a superhuman feat, holding back another deluge of tears. My throat ached with the strain. I said, 'I need something to help me sleep, so I don't have nightmares. And something for during the day, too. Maybe you could call my doctor.'

She was very pleased to have a task. It was as if I'd done her an enormous favour. I gave her my doctor's number and she promised to look after it first thing in the morning.

'If you give me your health card, I can pick up the prescription for you,' she offered. 'I'll bring it to you, shall I?'

I nodded, and tried to remember where I'd placed my wallet. How was it possible that I still had a wallet?

'I have an overnight bag in the car,' she said. 'I can stay here with you, we can sit up all night, or you can try to sleep. I don't like to think of you alone.'

She must have seen my dismay. A stranger in the house, a stranger who required civility. I was not up to civility. How could she ask this of me, ask anything of me?

'I need time alone,' I said.

She hastily agreed. 'Everyone's different,' she said. 'Some people are helped by being left to themselves for a bit, others find it helpful to have some company. Please call me any time you need to talk, night or day. Even if it's three in the morning.'

She hesitated. There was one more thing on her agenda, one more item to tick off, and she didn't know how to broach it.

I shook my head. 'I need to take care of my son's cat,' I said.

The bereavement woman smiled sadly. 'Pursie's a winsome cat,' she said.

After she left I taped a sign to the door, scrawled in black marker:

PLEASE RESPECT MY PRIVACY

PLEASE LEAVE PACKAGES ON THE DOORSTEP

When the bereavement woman shut the door behind her, I realized I hadn't thought about my birthmark during her visit. The stain on my face, which had seemed so important all these years, so all-consuming, had dissolved into nothing.

Many things had been important: the state of Neil's house, my son's school projects, an overdue fine at the library.

Now there was nothing I had to care about, was able to care about. The only task was to stay alive. It would be a massive, unfathomable effort.

If only there were someone else to take care of Pursie!

Of course, had parasitic Sherry and her clockwork-orange children not landed on Neil's doorstep, bringing havoc with them, Neil could have taken our son's cat.

One more reason to despise her.

———

I knew I had to eat, though nausea continued to gnaw at my stomach.

I bit into one of the cookies that the bereavement woman had left for me. It was too sweet, too bland, too dry, but I managed to swallow it.

I was afraid to go back to sleep. I remembered that my son and I had taken out a DVD from the library. We'd watched it yesterday. Yesterday—the concept was hard to grasp. Yesterday was light years away, yesterday existed in another dimension. In that twilit zone we'd eaten homemade pizza while watching a video. My son loved those pizzas. He was in charge of toppings, and he kept trying new things. He was interested in food.

It came to me like a boxer's blow that I would never cook for him again. I could do nothing for him now. I saw the burgundy car hitting his body again and again.

I imagined myself stopping the car, shaking the driver so he'd wake up in time. Old Hiram's goat had stopped the train—*He coughed and coughed, in mortal pain, coughed up those shirts* ... I was losing my mind.

I found the remote and switched on the DVD player. Actors were moving and speaking, and as I stared at them, the madness receded, though it remained in the room, hovering at the edges, prowling the corners.

When the movie ended, I skipped back to the beginning. It was a murder mystery or thriller, and I watched it again and again, all night long. Nothing in the movie changed. The characters said the same things, in the same way, at the same locations. Nothing unexpected would happen in that world. No one young and innocent would suddenly die. And in the end, good triumphed over evil. It was the last movie my son had seen.

Lost and longing to die, I made it through the night. My jailer lay next to me and purred.

october

My days are entirely the same and entirely different. That is, each day must be endured, and the exertion makes every minute a new drama of anguish.

My mornings used to begin with coffee in the shed. We called it the shed because that's what it was when we came to live here—an ancient horse shed behind the house, a few yards from the back porch. As soon as we moved in, I found an odd-job man, and together we installed windows, a door, flooring, insulation. The horse shelter became my studio, the place where I painted, but my son and I continued to refer to it as the shed.

That part of my life no longer exists, and the shed might as well have been carried off by a tornado. There is nothing there that I need or want. I can't imagine why I ever bothered mixing paints, stretching canvases, trying to create something that was in any case never what I'd hoped it would be.

Instead I swallow a venom-green capsule, and carry the mug of coffee to my son's room. I am less afraid now of crossing the threshold into his bedroom, of breathing the air he breathed. My presence will not disrupt his enshrined world.

I lie down on the unmade bed, next to my son's silver laptop. It's been snapped shut, the laptop, its secrets locked away. Holding the mug in my right hand, I let the fingers of my left hand slide along its cool, polished surface.

The room seems to rein in my terror, or maybe the terror merely takes time to get going. Eventually, as the day slithers onward, it will insinuate itself into my being, keep me company until bedtime.

I stare at the floor-to-ceiling animal collage that decorates the walls. Farm animals, wild animals, insects, birds, reptiles. My son began working on the collage when he was seven, and four years later had not yet tired of it. Instead, he kept adding new pictures, though how he squeezed them in I'm not sure.

Tears, sobs, choking, keening come next. I would cry all day, but the partial inactivation of my serotonin mechanism kicks in, and the rest of the day is a blur.

I retreat to a world of make-believe. With Pursie curled up on my lap or stretching herself for a tummy rub, I sit in front of the television and seek escape. We never had cable, but I have a pile of DVDs from the library.

If the setting of the show or film I'm watching is pleasant, I hunger for what I see, I hunger to believe that these are not actors on a set, but actual people—Cambridge undergraduates, let's say—out punting along the River Cam on a cloudless day in spring. These are not costumes, the story is not invented. I long to find myself inside an imaginary world—touch the decorative bottles on the drawing-room windowsill, talk to Mr. Beebe. If, on the other hand, a scene is full of sorrow and danger, I want to be on the set, observing the cameras and makeup artists and lighting technicians manipulate the story. And all those dangers—accident, crime, disease—would be exposed as artifice.

Either way, I'd be there, not here.

And so, wrapped in my mauve mohair blanket, I spend long hours—the entire day, really—watching movies and television series.

Or else I watch *The Big Bang Theory*, because my son liked that show and owned the entire set. He had a crush on Penny, and blushed when I teased him about it. I watch the same episodes again and again. I try to remember what my son said about them. He only liked some episodes, some scenes. Which ones? A week before he died he wrote to CBS to complain about insensitive and even cruel references to animals on the show. He asked me to look at the letter and correct any mistakes he'd made. He was a fan, he told CBS, but he did not think the characters would be so ignorant about animal rights, and so indifferent to animal suffering. I told my son that networks took their advertisers into consideration and he accused me of making excuses for them.

He was an idealist, my son.

I saw an Italian film once, about a woman who moves from a reality in which she has lost her husband, to one in which he is still alive and they have a child. Back and forth she staggers, dizzy and traumatized, unable to hang on to the life she's recovered, never knowing when she'll be flung back into loss.

That is what it's like, each time I leave this house. I enter another dimension, one in which my son never existed at all. In that faceless, anonymous universe, even his absence does not exist. My loss is confined to these four rooms. His things are here, his DNA is here.

His DNA—maybe one day I'll be able to clone him from his hair, his skin! I must collect his hair! I must find whatever strands I can, on his pillow, his hairbrush—I must freeze them in a baggie—or maybe there's a lab that will take his DNA, keep it safe. And one day, when the cloning of humans is allowed, I'll have my son back, and not only that, I'll have the past eleven years with him all over again—

Reason lunges out at me like a lasso through fog, hauls me back to reality, and I sink down to the sofa, unable to move. My fantasies are the agonies of Tantalus: I reach out and encounter nothing.

The leaves are turning. I lower my blinds against the glowing forest, the clear blue sky. I don't want to see what my son can't see.

Such emptiness.

When my son was alive, there was always some exciting quandary to tackle.

The chemicals in the pool made him itchy.

His classroom was too hot.

A gadget broke. It was still under warranty but in the meantime a new model had come on the market—would the store agree to an exchange?

His friend Elias, whose parents belonged to a clandestine cult, had written a composition about suicide that worried us.

Two friends had asked him to join them for Halloween at different locations, what should he do? He wanted to dress up as a herbivorous Neanderthal—how could he convey that?

Should I drive him to Toronto to see his grandmother, or should Neil, who would be asked to run errands for his mother-in-law and fix things in her house but wanted to take our son to the new Science Centre exhibition?

How would we celebrate his birthday this year?

How about if we drove to the farm to make sure the eggs came from well-treated chickens?

He had a cold but didn't want to miss cross-country skiing with his friend Mark.

He had dry elbows.

Should we invite someone to come with us to Stratford this year? Which plays looked good?

What if he and Mark started laughing again during the two minutes of silence on Remembrance Day?

Did his letter to the editor sound too bossy?

Would I read the spoiler on Wikipedia and tell him if the movie had a happy ending?

He'd lent *Labyrinth* to Adina and she still hadn't returned it. Should he give up and buy the film on eBay or had he outgrown it anyhow?

What was the difference between 'continual' and 'continuous'?

Would getting a prize make him more popular or less popular?

Where was Pursie hiding her cat toys?

Yes, it was his turn to do the litter this week. And could he please not leave the scooper in the litter box, or his shoes right in the middle of the mat, or empty containers of milk and yogurt in the fridge, because how will I know that we're out?

What I'm trying to say is that my days were filled with parenting. It was a fun pastime. I had created a person and then I created a home. I was playing house and it turned out to be my favourite game.

At the back of my mind, the nagging feeling that I've forgotten to do something persists—the last throes of habit. I held in my hand the millions of kite strings that connected my son to the world. Now, suddenly, the strings have slackened and slipped from my hands. This is not one ending, but a million endings. Each one batters me. How can I survive the gauntlet of these losses? How?

———

I am drawn into the past—another escape hatch. The venom-green pills slow me down, and I feel myself changing gears. It is as if the drug has drawn me out of the icy waters and dumped me in a boat, swaddled me with blankets. Mummified inside this vessel, I need not struggle against the waves. They carry me where they will, and the pain that now defines me is frozen and mute.

———

All is chance. My son's conception was as unlikely as his death.

If I had not picked up Toronto's alternative weekly at the grocery store—if they'd run out of copies, for example—or if an ad for art classes had not caught my eye—

BEGINNERS, INTERMEDIATE, ADVANCED.
WORLD-FAMOUS ARTIST OFFERING COURSES
IN DRAWING AND PAINTING.
MONDAYS AND WEDNESDAYS AT 7 P.M.

An unnamed artist, a derelict corner of the city, and the back pages of *Now*, right next to the psychics and mistresses of discipline—it all seemed made to order for me. I had my fine arts degree by then, but I'd been writing school textbooks for a living, and I was attracted to the idea of painting again, especially in a makeshift setting that seemed as far removed as one could hope from the strain of academia. I was curious, too, and I wanted to support the person behind this touching solicitation.

Or was it the ghost of my son, waiting to be born, that directed me to Mademoiselle Katyenka's art classes?

As it turned out, Mademoiselle Katyenka really had been a well-known figure in Russian Expressionism, once upon a time. She was in her seventies, mad and imperious and nearly useless, but many of the students were as mad as she was, and the clash between the intimate atmosphere and the Kafkaesque setting—the classes were held in an abandoned factory—inspired me, and I began experimenting with new styles.

Neil was by far the best student in the class. Everyone knew it, apart from Neil himself. He hated everything he did, tore up and crumpled work of great beauty, and I had to rescue the sheets from the garbage, smooth them out, take them home. They looked even better taped up and crinkly, and I imagined collecting enough of these discards to mount an exhibition. 'Rejects,' it would be called. Mademoiselle Katyenka often addressed Neil as 'Young Werther.' 'I'm nothing like Young Werther,' he protested comically. Mademoiselle Katyenka sighed and said, 'You are a genius, but you have no resilience.' She was lucid from time to time, in the midst of her ramblings. She wore paper flowers in her hair and often showed us the frostbite scars on her bare feet, which she said were a memorial to Stalin, though she didn't elaborate.

I was not inclined to speak to anyone. If I didn't interact with others, I would not have to witness their shock, politeness, confusion, distress, their patronizing determination to disregard one half of my face. I had a rimless felt hat that came down to my eyebrows and allowed me to imagine I was in shadow, and I wore my hair long and loose, but I knew there was no getting away from my stain.

It was Neil who finally approached me. He saw me retrieving his work, and asked me why I did it. He seemed genuinely puzzled. And because he was even more self-conscious than I was, and seemed not to notice anything peculiar about me, I looked up at him when I answered.

'Because you're throwing out really good stuff. If you don't want to keep it, I do.' Worried that I'd sounded defensive and, as usual, too intense, I added, 'One day it'll be worth a small fortune.'

Neil laughed. 'Good thinking. You'll be able to buy a Maserati with this evidence of my insanity.'

'Oh, are you insane?'

'What else would bring me here?'

My son's death changes not only the present and the future. It changes the past.

For years, the end of the affair with Neil was something wounding, providing secondary gains of self-righteousness and martyrdom, proving to me the hopelessness of my situation, adding to my treasured list of losses. I thought I knew what loss was. I didn't have a breath of an inkling.

It was a Wednesday evening in mid-August. I was pregnant and in love. Two months into Mademoiselle Katyenka's class, the old wooden stairway in Neil's East York apartment building had collapsed. I offered the spare room in my flat, because I liked him and because he had nowhere to go.

It was a convenient arrangement that turned into a relationship. But I don't want to dwell on those ten dewy-eyed months, not now.

I want instead to zoom in on that August evening. I was in my second trimester, and still making my way twice a week to Mademoiselle Katyenka's eccentric classes. Apart from the creative pleasure the classes provided, they had become a hideout where I could more or less disappear.

Neil no longer came with me. He'd started volunteering at an after-hours animal hospital, and in any case he'd given up on art. 'Katyenka's right,' he said. 'I don't have the stomach for regular servings of disappointment and defeat.'

On that Wednesday, for the first time ever, Mademoiselle Katyenka failed to show up. We would have probably gone ahead without her, but she had the key to the equipment closet. Without easels and utensils, there was nothing for it but to go home.

I couldn't remember whether Neil was at the animal hospital. Had I been sure, I'd have gone to visit him there. I liked seeing him in his white coat, communing with dogs and cats and the occasional rabbit. His cynical listlessness and moody distrust vanished, and he became gentle and even sentimental. He calmed anxious owners by reassuring their pets. 'What's ailing you, little fellow?' he'd say. A Neil I barely knew, but one who fed my projected image of him as a loving father. An image that proved to be accurate.

I didn't own a cellphone, and as Neil was not overly communicative about his erratic schedule or anything else, I biked home. I had not been sleeping well, and though it was early, I showered and went straight to bed.

The door to the bedroom was slightly open, and I was just drifting off when I heard Neil enter the apartment with his high-school friend Dominic. They'd been loners then and were loners still, each the only friend of the other.

They lit up, and I considered carting myself out of bed and shutting the door against second-hand cannabis smoke, but I was too sleepy. Their male voices reached me first as a murmur, and then, as inhibitions fell away, more clearly. I heard Neil say, 'Yeah, I don't know how it happened exactly. I found out I'm not the person I thought I was. I've been exposed as reprehensible. I felt bad for her, you know. But pity is so master-slave.'

Dominic laughed. 'Hegel? Hegel? Hegel?' he asked, in a crescendo of incredulity.

Neil said, 'All I know is, when we walk together, I pretend she's my sister or a distant cousin. I can barely eat with her, you know? Her face turns my stomach.'

'And you're having a baby together?'

'I know, I know. It was an accident. The whole thing was an accident.'

'I can't exactly picture you singing rock-a-bye-baby. When the bough breaks? What's that all about? Some sort of repressed infanticide fantasy? So what's next, house in suburbia? White-collar job? Two-car garage?'

'I like kids. Kids are wise.'

'Oh, I get it. Salinger throwback ... well, good luck. I'll send you the *Bhagavad-Gita* when the kid's born. You can read it to him at bedtime.'

I can't say it came out of the blue. I'd been aware of difficulties, but I had found a way to reformulate unsettling incidents. Cast them in a golden hue.

My love for my unborn baby usurped all other considerations. I said to Neil, 'We'll live on the same street. We'll have shared custody. We'll praise each other to our child. I'll say, Daddy's wonderful. And you'll say, Mummy's amazing.'

And that was that. Money was never discussed. We were both childishly generous, and we pooled what we had for the sake of our son. When I left the city, Neil followed me. His parents had died, and he inherited their Toronto house as well as their substantial savings, for though Neil's parents had been immigrants with modest jobs—his mother worked at a daycare, his father in shipping—they were the opposite of Neil and saved compulsively for their only child. The golden era of the sixties, when money seemed to grow on federal trees, helped them as well. I was not yet born, but my mother likes to reminisce about those days.

In any case, Neil sold the house for nearly fifty times its purchase price only three decades earlier. It was a windfall, and with the proceeds from the sale I bought this four-room cottage and Neil bought the clapboard house on Cityview Drive.

All these years, the overheard conversation between Neil and Dominic remained inert. I did not revisit it, I did not question it. But now I find that it has changed into something else, though I'm not sure what exactly.

I am too sick at the moment, bodily and otherwise, to unravel its new character.

Sickness suits me.

Food, for example. Everything I eat is too sweet, too salty, too bitter, too mushy, too tangy, too spicy, too taste-less, too revolting to swallow. Yet swallow I must.

I buy anything and everything. I fill my house with food that can be eaten straight from the container or requires only defrosting. The counter is piled high with chocolate, cashew nuts, bags of potato chips, cans of beans, wrapped bars. The fridge and freezer overflow with breads, cakes, dips, cheese, cherries, ice cream, organic frozen dinners.

The butter goes rancid, the fruit rots. I am wasteful. If my son were here he'd lecture me. But my son is not here.

It isn't only my taste buds that reject the food I eat. My stomach churns its contents too quickly, as if unable to take them seriously. I run to the toilet countless times each day.

Pursie stalks me. She always was a stalker, strategic-
ally placing herself within easy reach of a caressing hand.
It made us laugh, her stalking. When I showered, she
jumped on the ledge and peeked in through the curtain,
unafraid of the water. Closed doors made her anxious,
and when my son bathed, I had to distract her with extra
attention. But at the same time she was acquiescent in her
attention-seeking. If a caress was not forthcoming, she sat
patiently by our side until we moved again.

Now she follows me more than ever. I feel she's worried
about me, and doesn't know how to help.

This food that I buy—I buy it at the supermarket. The
supermarket is open all night, and its aisles are nearly
empty in the small hours, but the lure of nine hours of
unconsciousness is stronger than my aversion to the
featureless figures that surround me like holograms as I
shop.

I had a dream the day after my son died, a strangely
pleasant dream that came during an afternoon nap and
was no doubt set in motion by the emergency concoction
my doctor had prescribed. The venom-green capsules are
slow-acting, so she'd added two weeks' worth of a milder
but more immediately effective drug.

In the dream I was in a sci-fi control room when an
emergency siren went off. I ran to the door but it had

locked automatically, and I knew that we were doomed. I did not mind very much. There were only three of us in the room: myself, a tall, dark-haired scientist in a suit and tie, and another very faint male figure that I was not sure was there at all. The scientist was a stranger and rather formal, but I went over and held him, so we would not die alone.

But, remarkably, we did not die. We found ourselves transported instead to another planet, inhabited by beings who looked like benign and somewhat unkempt humans. *Shlumpy,* as my mother would have said. They glanced at us with mild curiosity, but when they tried to approach our capsule, they encountered an invisible but impenetrable wall. We were completely protected. I felt joyous about the invisible wall, joyous that I was safe.

In the past, the impenetrable wall was my despised stain. It stood between myself and everything I wished for: society, normalcy, lovers, fun. I had a son in spite of it—though my son was the most important prize of all, and overshadowed all other rewards.

Now I rely on my stain. It protects me from the hologram people pushing carts down the aisles of the supermarket. I am helped as well by self-checkout. In this case, the computer's voice is a huge relief. *Please place your next item on the scale-reader. Enter the number of bags and press done. Thank you for using self-checkout.* No questions asked, no answer required.

Fending off family members and sundry acquaintances has been a more complicated task. I thought no one would be so heartless as to deny me my one wish, now that I was bereft. I want to be left alone, that is all. Even condemned murderers are allowed to choose their last meal. And I have done nothing, or else I have committed a truly unspeakable crime, if just deserts are anything to go by.

But it was as if I had signed up to be an act in a freak show, as if what I most wanted was a steady stream of voyeurs. *Come see despair first-hand—reserve your tickets now*. Oh, the utter obtuseness of people!

My father, who died of advanced old age when my son was six, has been spared the death of his nth grandchild. Or perhaps it is I who have been spared the inadequacy of my father's response.

He was many years older than my mother, fifty-two when he married her, nearly sixty when I was born. My mother was his third wife, and I was his eighth child. Seven perfect children, and then me.

He taught sociology at a community college populated for the most part by high-school dropouts who looked as if they'd been clubbing all night and hadn't had time to change. There he met his first wife, Lise-Anne. She was chair of the department and a feminist pundit who appeared frequently on local television. She now has her own show, in fact: *Lise-Anne About Town*. With Lise-Anne my father had two sons and two daughters.

Billie, his second wife, was a former student. She was half-Jamaican, nineteen years his junior, pierced and tattooed and brazen when he met her, but transformed by her wedding into a conventional, community-oriented mother. My father and Billie had three daughters.

My mother was Billie's wedding planner. After the birth of her third daughter, or maybe long before that, Billie fell in love with a neighbour, and my father, who reacted to the news by tearing up his and Billie's wedding photos, suddenly remembered their charming wedding planner. Three months later, my mother was planning her own wedding.

My mother miscarried several times before giving birth to me, and did not try again after I was born. Maybe she feared my stain was genetic, or maybe the trauma of my stain—for it was her misfortune, not mine—discouraged her. In any case, I was the eighth of my father's children, and the last.

All this by way of explaining that I have seven half-siblings, most of whom have married and reproduced. I've lost count of their respective offspring, though they were my son's half-cousins. We were not in touch.

A large family, and at the same time no family at all.

———

And what of my mother, who has lost her only grandchild?

To answer this question I would have to spin myself back to my own childhood. I would have to write about what it was like, with my mother, right from the start.

At least writing is something to do. This dismal account, written to no purpose and for nobody, not even for myself, is the only thing that does not require a Sisyphean effort. Paying the gas bill, for example, all but flattens me. I must rip open the envelope with unwilling, inept fingers, I must locate the bank's website on my computer. When I reach it, I find myself staring blankly at the screen. I can barely muster the energy to type in my password—or remember it. I am as slow as a turtle, as slow as the living dead, risen from an everlasting grave.

It is in order to avoid trips to the bank that I have kept my computer and Internet service. I solved the email problem with Auto-Response, and all mail is now returned with the message: *This address is no longer valid.* The only letter I sent before exiting the site forever was the one informing my publishers and co-author that I would not be able to meet my current obligations. They will have to prepare the revision of our textbooks without me.

I would climb on the roof and shout out at my intruders: I am not being perverse! I haven't chosen to be isolated. I am isolated. The death of my son shipwrecked me on this island.

What I mean to say is that a feather would fell me, never mind a dagger. Why would I want to submit myself to additional torment? Why? In a sense, I am already at the bottom, and numb from the fall, but life is not that merciful. As long as I am alive, there is always room for one more stab.

This is the reason I have not opened the kryptonite cards and letters that have arrived in the mail. Nothing could induce me to read them. I haven't even looked at the return addresses. I was going to throw them all out, but in the end I tossed them under the kitchen sink, behind the garbage pail.

If I knew in advance what the letters contained, I wouldn't fear them. If I knew that they were not carrying stock messages of solace and hope, but confirmed instead that the loss of my son is unendurable and there is no way out—but I know that is not the case. No one has written, *Your life is no longer worth living.* Or, *How appalling that you have to carry on for the sake of the cat.* Or, *You must resent everyone who is still alive.*

It would be worse if I had to see these self-appointed comforters in person. I would not be able to tape their mouths shut, to block my ears. I would not be able to toss them under the sink.

Even the bereavement woman hurt me, with her hand-outs and books. I'd burn those books if I could be bothered.

And I'd have to consider their feelings, wouldn't I? But I'm wrung out, I'm out of commission, with nothing, absolutely nothing, in working order. How can I think of others when even breathing is hard work?

I confess there are times when I hate Pursie. I am wracked with guilt, not because of my hatred, which she knows nothing about, but because of my inability to speak to her.

I used to spill endearments at her with abandon. Truly over-the-top I was, with my billing and cooing, my long string of nonsense words, my silly baby voice. My son was too old to endure that sort of thing, but the need still flourished inside me, was near to bursting. And as I stroked Pursie's belly or her trembling old-man's chin, as I scratched her ears and cuddled her head against my throat, I smothered her in sweet talk that was at the same time directed, privately, at my son.

I had a friend, a neighbour, when I was ten, and the two of us would squeal every time we saw a cute animal. Our outbursts, which were tinged with pity, never failed to stir my father to sociological ruminations in which he tried to interpret what he considered our irrational solicitude for an evidently happy animal. We were not deterred, Selena and I. We continued to squeal and yelp at poodles and kittens.

If he were alive I would explain to my father that it is the vulnerability of an adorable pet that evokes concern along with delight. I have many such imaginary conversations with my dead father. I had them even when he was alive.

Does Pursie miss my voice? It's hard to tell with her. I feel guilty, but verbal expressions of love are simply beyond my power. It is too much to ask.

―――――

Am I ready to return to the subject of my mother, to step into that slippery mud-wrestling arena? If these bits of writing shorten my day by even half an hour, they are worthwhile. Time is my enemy.

I was supposed to be working on textbook revision this fall. I was getting ready to start when my son was killed.

Another chance event, my writing career. I never expected or planned to write textbooks, especially not in the field of genetics. I completed my fine arts degree only because I needed the student loans. Almost everything about the program—everything but the art itself, I guess—made me want to walk out and never return. The students lived in perpetual dread of being uncool, and the rules of coolness, which were set, as far as I could tell, by pseudo-gay nineteen-year-olds, oppressed and intimidated them and made them nasty and narrow. It could have been one long Milgram experiment.

But somehow I stuck to it. I even had sex in my first year, with a waif-like boy named Fede, but that's another story.

So, no convocation for me, but I graduated. I was wondering what to do next, given my reluctance to present myself at interviews. I might have girded my loins, hacked my way through the thicket, but in fact there were no jobs to apply for. Meanwhile I had to cover basic living expenses and repay student loans. Nursing bills and too many children had eaten up my father's resources, and my mother was not willing to help me. I considered cleaning offices at night.

Ms. Geri Wolfe came to my rescue. Really Dr. Wolfe, but she preferred Ms. She taught biology at Hawthorn, the private Catholic girls' school I attended, not because either of my parents was Catholic—though I did have a lapsed Catholic grandfather—but because it was the best place for someone like me.

Ms. Wolfe—I never could adjust to calling her Geri— had been asked to work on a new genetics textbook for high-school students, a textbook that was detailed and challenging, but at the same time easy to understand. She remembered my good grades and hoped I'd be interested in co-writing the book.

I wrote back to say that I wasn't qualified, but it turned out that the publishers wanted a lay person to be involved, someone who could look at the technical explanations with an outsider's eye.

Ms. Wolfe withdrew from the project halfway through the first draft. Her husband had died, and after forty years of teaching she decided to fulfill a lifelong dream and move to Greece. Another biologist took over, and together we completed the book. I ended up contributing illustrations as well.

My idea was to use cartoons. It was not an original idea—the image of sperm commenting on their race to the ovum is commonplace. I merely expanded it to talking chromosomes and talking receptor proteins. I also pushed for informal language, and rewrote nearly everything my co-author sent me. *When it comes to the sex cells in your body, the ones that are possibly going to form a new human ...'*

There were objections from some of the editors, who worried that the book didn't prepare students for the scientific style they'd encounter in university, or that students would confuse the molecules in their bodies with sentient beings capable of cognition. (Who was to say, I wanted to write back, that they were not?) But the mutterers were outvoted, and the book was a success. Teachers liked it, students liked it. Three years later, I worked on a second book for middle school. The royalties and annual revisions kept me afloat.

Recalling all this, I feel as if I am speaking of another person. I had a different identity then, a different brain. That former self is as unreal as a phantom. Or maybe that self was real and it is my present self that is dematerializing.

But at the same time—at the same time, the memory wrenches me and I feel I will drown in sorrow. My son, my brilliant son, watched me often as I worked. The subject matter, which he asked me to explain to him, captured his imagination. 'You mean all that is happening in billions of cells, right this minute? And we don't feel it—we don't even know? Weird.' His favourite part was the checkpoints, where errors in DNA are detected in a stop-go system. 'Draw the guy who signals trains,' he suggested. He was my cartoon editor. He told me which ones were lame and which ones worked. For the text, *This is true of all animals,* he asked me to draw a raccoon.

'Come back, come back, come back!' I cry out in the emptiness. I want to pull his clothes out of the closet and bury myself under them. I can't go on, I tell Pursie. She looks up at me, her cat's brain sifting the sound of my voice, and purrs.

Comatose sleep, and a new day in which I must feed Pursie and change the litter. She's an indoor cat. My son and I weighed the pros and cons of letting her out and concluded that too many dangers lurk outdoors, both for her and for the fragile bird population—though a bird would have to land between Pursie's ears, I think, for her to have a go. The odd-job man and I expanded and screened-in the back porch, and Pursie sits on a table there and looks out at the world.

Also today: a second visit from the police.

They came once before, the police, on the third or fourth day, because I refused to open my door to whoever was there. Lise-Anne, I think, or maybe one of her daughters—they all sound the same.

In any case, my visitor called the police and they announced themselves through the front door. I kept the chain on, drew the door back only an inch.

'Just checking that you're all right, Miss. Some people were concerned.'

I told them I didn't want any visitors and they apologized for disturbing me. God save the Queen.

There were other attempts to invade my house, invade my mourning. A few pursuers came to the door every few minutes, pounding and calling out my name, prowling around the house, tapping on windows, refusing to leave quietly. Others lay in wait, and I was trapped indoors. I watched the parked cars through the curtain, waited for their occupants to give up. I couldn't understand their determination. I still can't.

Not that I need to go out. Apart from alpine excursions to the supermarket and drugstore, and sometimes the library, I have no reason to leave my house. Like Pursie, I have become an indoor animal.

Imagine lying in wait, though! Imagine that sort of crass insistence! For it is not me they're worried about, but themselves. I am a chore they want to tick off their to-do list, their guilt list.

This time the police came because of the flowers.

People brought flowers at first. They left them on my doorstep or at the side of the road. At night I gathered the flowers and scattered them in a ring around the house. For the house had become my son's grave, his tomb. I thought of Ophelia, whose body I could have been inhabiting at that moment. I pictured her, not floating prettily amidst daisies and nettles, but grotesque and bloated, her fetus—are nettles not recommended for pregnant women?—trapped inside her. One fool had brought white roses and when I returned to the house I saw that my arms and hands were covered with blood.

Then the floral tributes trailed off and I stopped paying attention to the stray bouquets that still showed up. I wanted to despise them, but how can one despise flowers? Still, what good were they? What good did they do? They could not bring my son back.

But it seems that yesterday one of my stalkers noticed the wilted flowers on my doorstep and persuaded the police to pay a second visit.

They were less considerate this time. 'Well, clear them up,' they said. 'That way there won't be any mis-understandings.'

I have moved from bereaved citizen to nuisance. It didn't take much, did it? God save the Queen, but not the police.

What I am trying to say is that they did not love my son, these visitors. How can they have anything to say to me, when they did not love him? Only Neil and I loved him as he deserved to be loved.

And Neil has not come, nor will he come.

As soon as my son was born I understood the risk, the wild risk, I had taken. As soon as I held him in my arms, a great love flooded my being, love such as I'd never known, and I saw what I had done. What if I lost him, what then? By having him, I'd created that possibility, a possibility that had never existed before.

I handed him to Neil, who was afraid to take him at first, afraid he wouldn't know how to hold him. But everyone urged Neil on, and he gave in to pressure. He held his son and loved him as I did. His son who looked so much like him, even as a five-minute-old infant.

The anxiety never entirely left me, but at the same time, I'd grown overconfident. Statistics were in my favour. The world was filled with old people who had made it through the perils of life. I did not have to fuss each time my son climbed on his bike. Neil laughed at my worrying, and so did my son, and I began to worry less.

But they were wrong, weren't they? I should have

remained vigilant. I should not have trusted in chance for a single second, because a second is all it takes. How could I have left him alone in front of the house? What if a kidnapper had sped by, one of those psychotic criminals in the shows I now watch to pass the time? Shows that after all are based on things that happen, have happened.

I became blasé. I stopped pleading with the Fates from morning to night. That was my arrogant crime.

And another thing I want to know—in those shows I watch, the ones with depraved criminals, how is it that the day after a mother is informed that her child has died, there she is, in one piece, hair blow-dried, makeup on?

Is this TV Land or are some parents like that? Maybe they did not love their children all that much. It's a myth, that all parents love their children. For if the scale runs one to a thousand, some parents rate ten or a hundred only. Their love is wobbly, abstract. I am one to know—my mother's score bounced about, but I doubt she ever made it past the halfway mark.

Or maybe these mothers have other people in their lives, people who love them and need them and blow-dry their hair for them.

Or could it be that they are stronger than me, the parents who remain intact on the outside? Maybe maintaining a respectable front helps them in some way—promotes their privacy, if nothing else. I remember a caterer my mother worked with. Her daughter died, and yet she came to work a week later. Maybe she said to herself, 'Since I am forced to go on, I may as well cook.' And I imagine the rent had to be paid.

I don't have that sort of strength. I am barely able to lift a hairbrush. If I don't brush my hair, I will have to cut it all off, and I can't cut it, because my son loved what he called my fairy-gold hair, and he sometimes ran his fingers through it. They are holy, sacred, the things that he touched.

I do shower now and then. That is, I find myself in the shower, though I have no memory of taking off my clothes or turning on the water. Pursie startles me back to consciousness, hopping onto the bathtub ledge and peering at me from behind the curtain, her small mottled face earnestly expressive—though of what, I cannot say.

I was going to write about Selena, sweet Selena who squealed at cute animals with me, for she's been on my mind these past few days, though I haven't thought of her for years. My first friend, and my only friend, apart from, possibly, Fede.

But to write about Selena would mean dredging up my years at Hawthorn and suddenly I am so overwhelmed with disgust at myself that I want to vomit all over the keyboard.

What did it matter, that I looked as if one of my parents were a grape, as Selena put it. For Selena liked my face, she said it was interesting, different, made me unique. And then she said it looked as if I'd been born to a human and a grape, and we laughed until our bellies hurt.

But when my mother came home, Selena's words faded and I knew that I was not interesting and unique. I was deformed, and the way I looked made my mother cry.

I feel I am going to choke with rage and frustration. I had no pain, no illness, no limitations. I had nothing. I have nothing. Let my entire body be one large stain, and my son back. Let me have any affliction at all, and my son alive.

Nevus flammeus is its official name, and in my case it covers the left side of my face, though my stained skin is oddly smooth.

But so what? So what? It was my mother who turned it into a tragedy of epic proportions, it was the vanity of my parents that rubbed off on me. My son never noticed or cared. Why would anyone else who had half a brain?

Here is the truth about my Catholic schoolmates: I had a head start, because they were used to me, and because they'd been told to be nice by the highest authority of all. *God wants you to play with that girl.* My mother's motives may have been skewed, but her choice of school was a good one, and I remember being grateful that she and my father were willing to pay the high tuition fees.

But I squandered my head start. With confidence and the slightest hint of charm I could have transformed dutiful inclusion into real liking. My fellow students did not have only half a brain. They were ordinary. It was up to me, but I couldn't see it because I couldn't see that it didn't matter. I was misled by vanity—a word that means, appropriately, futility and waste.

Now that my insides are mauled and twisted, I prefer not to look like everyone else. I prefer to have my outcast state stamped on my face for all to see. Let the inside and outside match. And let bleak winter come and replace these sapphire skies, these scarlet leaves, which my son is not here to collect.

november

I've noticed lately one car that keeps turning up. It's stark white, and catches the green of the trees above it, for the driver parks on the opposite side of the road, under a row of pine trees.

It may be someone who rang the bell and received no answer. Someone I know, though I can't think who. It's too dark to see inside the car, and too far.

This is the most unrelenting of my visitors. The others have all vanished, no doubt in a cloud of relief. But whoever this is—is it one person, two?—they stay in the car sometimes for hours, though only on Wednesdays and Sundays, it seems. I am acutely aware of the days of the week, which I cross off on my real estate calendar, one by one, like the prisoner that I am. Each crossed-out day is a day less to get through. This sentence will end, eventually.

Images from my year with Selena paraded through my thoughts before I fell asleep last night. And this morning, as I lay on my son's bed in a reverie, she drifted in again.

These daydreams come upon me like a spell, not relieving grief but scrawling over it, so that I have something else to occupy me. In some daydreams my son is at Neil's, or at school, and will return soon. In others, I slip into the distant past, before I gave birth, before I met Neil.

I was ten when Selena moved in across the street with her mother and baby brother. They rented a ramshackle place, or maybe they were house-sitting. In any case, I think I knew from the start that it was a temporary arrangement.

Shady people had lived there before them, people in leather vests who, whether twenty or sixty, would always look young. They were in and out all day, these characters, in various combinations, so that we never knew who actually owned the house and who was visiting. The property was overrun with garbage and weeds, but no one dared complain. We were afraid of their dogs, for one thing. The dogs, too, seemed to change all the time.

My parents squabbled about these neighbours. My mother hated them outright, called their house a blight and an eyesore, and wanted to report them for violating city bylaws.

My father disagreed with her. In long-winded, theoretical arguments he defended them, maintaining that they were merely displaced. When he passed the house, if they were on the porch or front lawn, he went out of his way to wave hello or comment on the weather. They returned his greeting by raising their cans of beer or pop.

This was not out of character, for my father campaigned relentlessly on behalf of immigrants, for example. He set up grassroots committees, organized volunteer networks for newcomers, fought to have their qualifications recognized. And not only immigrants—he championed a whole series of causes for those on the fringe. He joined expeditions to lay water pipes in isolated villages across the globe, and enlisted my mother to plan fundraising events.

That was one side of my father. A different side emerged when Selena entered our lives.

The leather-vested men had vanished on a rainy November morning, and that afternoon Selena's mother moved in with her two children. I couldn't see then what I know now—how poor they were, for one thing. And Selena's mother—today I would recognize her as the sort of woman who adopts some kind of alternative persona but is really nothing more than half-crazy, making every wrong decision that a person can possibly make. The sort of woman who tells herself, in the midst of the chaos of her life, that it all makes sense because she cultivates yogurt.

Selena was the opposite. She was unnaturally sane, for a child—maybe because someone had to be.

She must have seen me coming home from school, though I didn't see her. I walked to my house with my head lowered, eyes on the sidewalk, hair cascading around me and eclipsing, I hoped, my face. I had just emptied my schoolbag on the carpeted floor of my bedroom when the doorbell rang. My mother was on the phone and I had no choice but to answer the door myself. Selena smiled at me and asked if I wanted to play cards. She held out the pack in her hand like a peace offering.

I waited for the punchline, but none came. Warily, I invited her inside. She was far too thin, but she was tall and quick, and her dark hair fell in perfect columns to her shoulders.

Our friendship was sealed that first afternoon. When I came home from Hawthorn, Selena would be waiting on my doorstep—the public school she went to was closer than mine and let out earlier—and she usually stayed for supper, though she was too polite to eat very much. She had perfect table manners—I don't know where she'd picked them up. I wanted her to move in with us on weekends, but she had to help with the baby. I don't think she trusted her mother to look after him properly, and we often crossed the street to change his diapers and feed him. What was his name? I can't recall.

It was impossible not to like her, and yet my father disliked her. It was snobbery. He could find no obvious fault with Selena. Instead, he adopted an all-knowing, faintly contemptuous attitude towards her, which he modified—or made worse—with self-congratulatory tolerance. When I spoke of her, he smiled with secret superiority.

That was the other side of my father. I understood even then that he suffered from the irrational humiliation of not having found a university job and not having had his one book noticed. He reshaped his self-doubt and consoled himself with his wives, his children, and his snobbery.

But there was more to it. Yes, he knew where Selena came from, and where, he assumed, she was headed, and he thought her background made her suspect. But his evidence was my appearance. He could not believe Selena had sought me out without ulterior motive. How could anyone accept me, when he himself found it so hard?

But now I ask myself—did my father truly love any of his children? And if he did, if he loved Lise-Anne's children and Billie's daughters, is it not possible that he was too dispirited, after those failed marriages and the loss of custody, to hazard parental attachment one more time?

I search for clues. All his women were beautiful. Once I overheard him comment to a group of friends who'd come for dinner that, had his wives not been good-looking, he would not have been interested in them. They were discussing criteria of attraction across cultures, and he was, as always, trying to prove a point. I don't know what the point was. I only heard that bit from the kitchen, where I was helping myself to leftovers.

I don't have an answer. It doesn't matter anyhow.

———

I was crying in the shower and it seemed to me that I had reached the end. I ran out into the night, wet and naked under my coat. I lay down on the rough, weedy grass between the back porch and the shed. I was shivering but I didn't feel cold. I looked up at the black sky, the stars, the unknowable infinite universe, and asked my son to allow me to find a home for Pursie. In the cold night I begged him to release me.

But I knew what he would say. An unspoken deathbed promise—*Take care of Pursie. Take care of Pursie.*

Too weak to stand, I crawled back to the house, crawled into my son's bed. Pursie, oblivious, slid under the blankets, out of sight, and began playing with a stray sock. Her tail tickled my legs and the blanket bulged here and there, as if alive. We would have had one of our laughing fits, if my son were here. Or I would have. That is one of the things I used to do—laugh helplessly, unable to stop. 'Get a grip, get a grip,' my son would say. 'Get a grip, Mom.'

———

Sins are like potatoes left in the ground, half-covered in earth, barely distinguishable from earth, hard and round and grey. Where did I read that? Or was it a film I saw, or a dream? A deserted field, a war maybe, and then winter descending, and the potatoes turning hard as ice, they'd be hard and cold against the soles of your feet if you stepped on them. And you can't walk anywhere without coming across them—two where you thought there was one, thousands where you thought there were a few.

Once, when my son was five, I lost my temper. I was driving on the 401 and he was in his child's seat in back, my briefcase beside him. Bored, he reached inside, took out my wallet and began removing everything—money, cards, slips of papers, receipts, appointment reminders. Then he turned the briefcase upside down and my genetics notes and drawings flew out.

I had told him many times not to play with my wallet and briefcase. Anything else I owned he could consider his.

But, as I said, he was bored. Maybe I forgot his CD. Or maybe music was not enough. When I glanced in the mirror and saw everything scattered in confusion behind me, I pulled over to the side of the highway and yelled at him. 'How many times have I told you, how many times?'

Of course my outburst had nothing to do with him. Another day I would have shaken my head, sighed, maybe even laughed. 'Not again,' I would have joked. 'Oh no, not again.'

But other troubles bore down on me—Neil, and my ailing, ninety-four-year-old father, and my exasperating, egocentric mother, and a power-hungry, alcoholic editor who had tried to hurt me that morning at a meeting and had succeeded. It was at that meeting that I decided to move out of the city.

I don't remember why we were on the 401 or where we were going. I knelt on the floor of the car and grumpily collected my things. I made my son feel bad, my wonderful son who was so easy and cooperative and thoughtful and relaxed, and here I was betraying him and scaring him even though I was the one who had left the briefcase within his reach. Only when I saw the tears streaming down his cheeks did my anger collapse. I apologized profusely, kissed him, wiped his nose.

I deserve the torment of that memory.

I wonder what became of Selena. Shortly before the end of the school year she told me they were moving to Alberta. We both cried and hugged each other. She promised to send me her address and phone number when she moved, but nothing arrived. I should have given her a stamped, self-addressed envelope—she was only in grade four. But I didn't think of it because I was ten years old. And my parents didn't think of it because they didn't care.

We had old-fashioned fun. Computers had not yet

invaded our daily lives, back in 1981. Do girls today play as we did? I don't know. I did most of my homework at school, during lunch, and the rest I dashed off before bed. Selena never seemed to have any homework at all. My mother kept more than a hundred bottles of nail polish in her room, and we'd sneak them out in handfuls and paint each of our toes and fingernails a different colour. We leafed through magazines for the pleasure of our running commentary. *Oh, cute. Oh, yuck.*

I had a large collection of art supplies, thanks to birthday and holiday and guilt gifts. I could have exploited my parents' occasional pangs of guilt, but gambled instead on wanting nothing—their love was the Holy Grail, not pastels. If I wanted nothing, would they love me more? I never stopped trying. Still, I was grateful for the clay and paints and sparkles.

Selena was obsessed with butterflies on flowers. That was all she ever wanted to draw, and that's what she begged me to draw for her again and again: a butterfly balanced on the petal of a flower. I obliged, and she'd kiss me once on each cheek to thank me for the present. Like her table manners, she'd picked up that polite kiss some-where. At the bottom of each page I'd write, *for Selena from her loyal friend Elise.*

What else? Oh yes, we played board games my grand-parents had given me over the years. My mother's parents, who seemed to think I had someone to play with. I did, in fact: I had a series of teenaged babysitters, and since we had no TV—my father could not abide television—we'd spend the evenings going through the games in my closet.

Most of the games were new to Selena, and I had to teach her the rules. We were world champions at Chinese Checkers, Snakes and Ladders, Clue, Enchanted Forest, Careers, Sorry!, Monopoly, and our favourite, Guess Who? The goofy characters of Guess Who? sent us into paroxysms of laughter. Selena called bald Herman my boyfriend and I retaliated by referring to pointy-headed Bill as hers. We had stories about them all. Philip still wet his bed, Claire sucked her thumb at night, Alfred was a druggie.

I gave Selena the Guess Who? set as a going-away present, and when my son was little we tried to find the game for him, but the company had replaced the comical faces with the worst type of generic cartoons. The names had changed too: Maria was now Ashley, Herman was Zachary. The game had been ruined. I ranted all the way home from the store. A phobic culture, I told my son, afraid of imagination and art, degrading everything into the ugliest, most one-dimensional form possible, it was a fundamentalist's dream—I caught myself, for I was sounding like my father.

My son was competitive when we played those games, and hoorayed when he won: Neil's influence, no doubt. Neil, unlike me, never intentionally let him win. The most he'd do was play with a handicap. After that it would be male to male, victory or defeat.

Selena did not play to win. She didn't care, and moved her pieces without strategy or forethought. When I commented on her artlessness to my father, hoping to impress him, he sneered. 'Of course she isn't trying to win,' he said. 'She wants to stay for supper. Smart cookie.' In fact Selena didn't have a cunning bone in her body. And if survival was connected in her mind with being generous and likeable, I could hardly fault her for that. Yet my father did.

And now my father is gone and Selena—I don't know where she is. Suddenly I remember her brother's name: Sebastian. How could I have forgotten? She talked about him all the time, as if he were her child rather than her brother.

Selena and Sebastian Blanco. I would have looked them up, had I thought of it before. I'd have taken my son to meet them and their children, if they had any. And then everything would have been different, and my son would not have been crouching on the grass at that moment, because if you change one thing, everything changes, and my son might still be alive.

The white car is here again, parked as always on the other side of the road, under the pine trees.

Is this the anonymous caller who contacted the police to report the wilted flowers? It must be someone who lives close by. Yet I can't think who I know from around here, other than Neil. I had only minimal contact with my son's teachers, or with other parents.

Well, fuck him, whoever he is.

Let's talk about Sherry today. Why not?

It seems extraordinary to me that I can string words together, that I still know how to type. These jottings on the screen, they're an act of desperation, a reflex response to the excruciating loneliness that runs rampant in these four rooms. Not even four: the kitchen and living-room are open concept, with only a counter to set them apart. I wander from my dark bedroom—I haven't raised the blinds since my son died—to my son's room, which is flooded with light, then back to the main room. I gave my son the large front room and took the small back one for myself. He was the one who needed the space to expand. And Neil, though we never discussed it, did the same when he bought the house on Cityview Drive—he gave our son the master bedroom with the ensuite bathroom. I forgot about that, because it became irrelevant soon after, when Sherry moved in.

I walk back and forth, back and forth, not so much pacing as searching in a daze, as if hoping that in the next room life will change, it will all have been a dream. *And then she woke up.* I lie on my son's bed, my head on his pillow, and stare at his animal collage. I keep seeing new animals—a snail I hadn't noticed, or a ruby-throated hummingbird. I collect stray strands of hair, dark and wavy like Neil's. I caress my son's silver laptop. He was secretive about that laptop, always shutting it quickly when I came too close, or moving it so I couldn't see the screen. I assumed he was checking out sex sites, for he was nearing puberty. He'd have been twelve in December.

I don't want to go mad, though I know I'm already halfway there. A line from an old Joan Baez song keeps coming to me: *sadness broke finally into madness.* Right now the venom-green pills are the only thing standing between me and irreversible mental illness. I could kill Sherry, for example. Good thing we have gun control in this country.

It would make more sense to stick to the original plan, if this is where I'm headed, for who would look after Pursie if I lost my mind? Yet this loneliness threatens my sanity. There was no one else in my life, only my son, and now there is no one.

My son was such good company. And though it hurt him that once Sherry had installed herself in Neil's house he could no longer stay there, or even visit, and it hurt me that he was hurt, it meant that I saw more of him. Neil picked him up from school, and they'd go to Starbucks for a snack and then to the new library branch to do homework and read newspapers. Newspapers! They liked to read the articles together, and they'd talk about politics and what was happening in the world. On weekends Neil took our son swimming, or shopping for a new bike, or just along on various errands. There was always somewhere to go. But he lived with me.

We talked. We had conversations, real conversations that were full of pondering and exploration. I visited one of my half-sisters once, for the sake of my son. Let him have some family, I thought. I chose the most likely candidate: Billie's middle daughter, Poppy, whom I'd run into at our father's nursing home. She worked for an arts council, and we discovered a shared love of modern dance. We reeled off names of choreographers and companies, for we were both excited to find a fellow aficionado. She lived in a rambling Victorian house in Ottawa, and she invited us to come and stay for the weekend.

The visit was not a success. Poppy turned out to be high-strung and controlling, and we felt ourselves disappearing inside the jet of anxiety that was her home life. But what struck me most was that my half-sister didn't converse with her children. She gave instructions, issued directions, discussed what needed to get done, but it didn't occur to her to share her thoughts with them, though the youngest was seven and the eldest fourteen. I shared my thoughts with my son even when he was in kindergarten. He always had such interesting things to say. About Poppy he mused, as we drove home, 'It's like she's the sun and everyone else is a little star. She's bright, but you can't really get close to her.'

Now I want to tell my son about his death and what it's been like without him. I want to explain about the visitors I refuse to let in, about the Catholic girls who could have been my friends, about Selena. If only I believed that he can hear me still. But the house is silent.

Oh, child psychiatrist, whose name I try to block out of my mind, whose name does not deserve residence in my brain, what a remarkable human you have killed!

These scenes I summon, of Neil and our son reading the newspaper in the library together, or having an after-school snack at Starbucks—sometimes I can't grasp that it's over and I see them there still. There are times when the finality is real, but at other times I coast. The brain can only support so much reality, it seems, before it shuts down and refuses to proceed.

Is that the meaning of mercy—drugs, illusion, sleep?

Where was I?

Oh yes, Sherry.

Though Neil was twenty-eight when we had sex, he'd only had two one-night stands before me. He was passive in bed, passive about sex in general. He said he'd never had much of a libido.

If I'd met him earlier, I would have attributed his sexual apathy to his past, but I knew more about the body by then, about the millions of biochemical events—most still barely understood—that contribute to what we think of as our personalities. Maybe something happened to Neil early on, but it is also possible that he was born that way.

Not that he had difficulty becoming aroused. But it was obvious that he would have preferred a less strenuous activity, or one that was not quite as loaded with intimation, not to mention intimacy. Even after I heard him tell Dominic that I repelled him, I believed he'd told me the truth about his indifference to sex. Neil was nothing if not honest. I asked him if he'd ever been attracted to Dominic, who slightly resembled Larry of *The Three Stooges,* and he chuckled. 'If I were gay,' he said, 'I don't think Dominic would be my first choice.' What Neil seemed to want most of all was to be on his own.

And yet, one day, not long after we moved out here, he logged onto a dating site. It was wildly out of character, but Neil was out of his element. He'd always been an urban guy, and I'd forced him to leave Toronto. He missed the camouflage of city grunge, and he missed getting together with Dominic for a round of pool, followed by a meal at an obscure Indian restaurant.

Neil felt shielded by the anonymity of the heavily populated metropolis: he was not alone but at the same time he didn't have to relate to anyone. Small-town Ontario was foreign territory. He complained about the quiet, the sameness, the courtesy. He never stopped shaking his head at the use of the word 'downtown' to refer to the five by four blocks that comprised a bus station, a train station, City Hall, and a few dozen stores.

For a while Neil made do with having his son nearby. He also liked living next to a nature reserve and witnessing the canine ecstasy of Ursula and Gudrun, his retriever-mix rescue dogs, at the mention of the word 'reserve.' Once or twice a month he drove into Toronto to hang out with Dominic.

But he was thirty-six, and maybe he decided that he'd been alone too long—all his life, not counting the apparently repugnant ten months with me.

And so, one night, on a whim, he Googled 'online dating' and clicked on the first address that showed up. He was too new to the phenomenon to realize he'd landed on one of the sleazier sites.

I used to say to our son, 'One day someone will discover that Dad can't say no, and that will be the end.'

When I said it, I pictured a layabout male friend who kept borrowing money. Neil gave to whoever asked, and though I was almost as hopeless in my easy and I suppose utopian approach to money—always wanting to fix, if I could, whatever needed fixing—I did draw some lines. Neil's lines were fuzzy, if they existed at all.

I joked about it, but I did not really believe it would happen. And even in my most pessimistic projections, I didn't envision a woman who'd logged onto lavalife.com in search of room and board and, if possible, a van.

Neil, who was usually so sharp, was taken in. Zelig-like, Sherry adopted his views and went one further. With convincing effusiveness she listed her serendipitous achievements. She had captured and neutered all the cats in her neighbourhood. She had distributed flyers for the NDP during the last elections, though really she was an anarchist. She agreed that the problem with so much contemporary art was that you can't be witty in the same way ten thousand times—that's exactly why she had quit her ceramics workshop. *Quelle coincidence!*

I think Neil, who would have faced a firing squad for his principles, was incapable of discerning feigned ideals in anyone else. It was so crude it worked.

Still, he didn't want her in his home. He'd meant only to go on a few dates so he'd have someone to talk to, other than me and our son. But a month into those dates Sherry announced that her landlord had thrown her out, and she and her two children were now homeless. Could she stay with him just until she found a new place?

But this is coming out all wrong. 'She can't help who she is,' my son said, in response to my frustration.

He was right, as always. Sherry is more lost than sly. She can't help who she is.

For a long time after our son was born I wasn't sure how I felt about Neil. I still worried about him, and I still found him attractive. I wondered whether, in spite of his betrayal, I still loved him. It was hard for me to wade through the tangled emotions that connected us. He was the wonderful father of my child.

It wasn't until I heard that Neil was dating that I knew my love for him had evaporated. Romantic love, anyhow. I was happy for Neil and happy for our son. A woman, I thought, would bring some much-needed spark and cheer into his life, not to mention window curtains. Curtains!

Sherry and her two children, then eight and ten and already terrifying, moved into Neil's two-storey house— or three storeys if you count the attic.

Apart from her children, Sherry brought with her four parakeets and several hundred boxes into which she'd stuffed every piece of paper, clothing, and miscellaneous object that had ever made its way into her life, including thousands of magazines and ten industrial-sized bags of lentils and beans that she'd won as a door prize at a church bazaar. It wasn't so much that she was attached to her belongings, as far as my son and I could tell. It was the prospect of sorting through the mess that defeated her.

The legumes turned out to have mouse droppings in them, and many of the boxes had been invaded by moths and silverfish. The magazines smelled of cat urine.

Sherry couldn't cope. Clothes weren't washed because the washing machine was buried under mounds of trash.

There was no linen on the beds and the uncovered pillows she and Neil slept on looked as if they'd been pulled out of a coal pile. Neil's cleaning woman quit, and the sinks and toilet bowls were soon coated with rust and grime. Food rotted in unknown places. It was impossible to cook so Sherry ordered out. Too lethargic to throw out the fast food containers, or unable to find garbage bags, Sherry left them where they were. Neil let the parakeets out of their cages when the dogs were in the yard, and bird excreta soon covered everything in sight. Neil began to look like a street person.

Sherry had an ex-husband in Kitchener. Her children could have made a fuss and gone to live with their father, but he had a new family, whereas Neil was the goose with the golden eggs. Suddenly it was Christmas every day.

Sherry's children have had, I assume, a sad life, and I want to believe that they are not beyond help, but no one seems to have tried. They release their hostility indiscriminately, intimidating not only other children but also adults. Some bullies confine themselves to easy targets, but Sherry's children sniff out vulnerability, no matter how well-concealed, and charge, casually aiming for the jugular. There's a physical element to their belligerence, for they hit each other constantly and radiate an air of boldness, but their method of choice is affectation and scorn. The affectation they learned from their mother. I don't know where the scorn came from.

Neil made no effort to control or influence Sherry's children. It's hard for me to write their names. Amy, Karl. They bullied our son, but they also bullied Neil—not into giving them what they asked for, which he did anyhow, but by poking fun at him.

I knew from our son that Neil had given Sherry his credit card and bought her a van. I think Sherry's use of the word 'anarchist' to describe herself really did pre-date Neil, who was far too jaded to align himself with any particular movement or ideology. For Sherry, a philosophy that ostensibly justified her various deficiencies must have seemed like a godsend. It was sheer luck, from her point of view, that she'd hit upon a concept that interested Neil, and that he didn't care whether or not she had any clue what it meant. My son described Sherry's visits to the supermarket. Unable to organize her thoughts, she threw items randomly into her shopping cart until it was full. The perishables perished, the non-perishables vanished in the vortex. Within two years of Sherry's arrival, Neil was barely managing to pay the utility bills.

Sherry claimed that she was unable to find work. More likely, she was unable to tear herself away from Facebook, to which she was addicted. She spent the entire day snacking on organic chocolate and communicating with her Facebook contacts. I sometimes read her nonsensical postings via my son's account. *Is a bird a symbol of empty flying or trying to get shot down by a teeming crowd?* Now and then I recognized, in distorted form,

Neil's ideas. *Ethel Rosenberg, yeah, revolutionary souls, go sistah!!* She was pretentious, but in a naive way—she was trying to fit in.

Neil had let a disturbed woman into his life and was apparently unwilling or unable to extricate himself. Why? No one ever found out.

I began to understand that all was not well with Neil, or rather, that more was wrong than I'd been willing to acknowledge. And yet when we spoke on the phone or in person, he seemed so rational, so reasonable.

He was a mystery, from start to finish.

december

I saw Neil today, as I was pulling into the supermarket's parking lot. I thought it was a mirage at first. Why would Neil be here, at this supermarket? His house is at the other end of town.

But it was him, though I could see only his back. I recognized his posture, his black Mazda, and there were Ursula and Gudrun, sitting upright in the back seat and gazing stoically at their protector's departing figure. I parked as far away as I could and slid down in my seat. He probably had an errand in the vicinity and was stopping to buy something on the way. The dentist, for example, had her office in this shopping centre.

I remained crouched in my car, hiding. Every now and then I peeked up to check if the black Mazda was still there. Finally, Neil returned with two bags of groceries.

I caught a glimpse of his face as he loaded the bags in the trunk. It wasn't him at all. It was Neil, but his features have changed.

Now I think I must have dreamt the entire thing.

I drove to Cityview Drive yesterday to spy on Neil. I parked at the end of the block and waited. Sherry's van was in the driveway, but not the black Mazda. I waited for hours. Amy and Karl came home from school, looking as surly as ever. They began punching each other as they approached the house, then moved on to kicking. How did Neil, who abhorred violence of any kind—who couldn't even watch violent films—cope with their fights? He must have blocked it all out. He always was good at blocking things out.

I waited until dark, and still Neil didn't come. It suddenly occurred to me that maybe he no longer lived there. It would be what Neil would do. He'd give Sherry the house and leave.

Too late now, Neil. Too late! If you'd loved your son you would have found a way to get rid of her long ago. And you would have told Amy and Karl that if they continued to bully your son they'd have to leave. Instead you let them hurt him, your only son, and you bought them presents and took them to restaurants.

You used all three of them as a weapon against your son, against me. You didn't love him. You didn't love him enough.

Death brings merciless clarity.

I'm wondering why Neil, if he's really left Sherry, has not returned to Toronto. His main source of income is work he does from home—something to do with computer engineering. He can live anywhere, so why is he still here? Maybe I'm mistaken and he hasn't left her. Maybe he was simply not home when I went to spy on him. He may have been visiting Dominic, or helping out at the local animal clinic. What does it matter, anyhow? Nothing connects us now.

The bereavement woman slid a card under my door this morning. A card with a delicate drawing of daffodils, and a handwritten note inside: *Please don't hesitate to call at any time, Elise. A counsellor is ready and waiting for you. We also have other programs that may help. We don't want you to feel alone.*

Followed by her name, which I forget.

Before Neil there was Fede—pronounced, idiosyncratically, to rhyme with *feed*. He was an elfin creature, a sort of Ariel, though with a somewhat larger head than you'd expect on such a slender body.

He was studying journalism and photography, and one of his electives was an art class I was taking. It was my first year at university, his second.

He painted me. We had some assignment or other, I forget what exactly, and he did a full-body portrait of me on a door-sized canvas. You couldn't tell I had a stain, because stains were part of the overall concept. I had huge ears in the painting, and antennae, and I was naked apart from a crimson coronation mantle.

Tears came to my eyes when he showed it to me, and for a few moments I couldn't speak at all. He made me a present of the painting and I still have it, wrapped in brown paper and plastic sheets, in my closet.

He was a Basque from New Brunswick. His parents ran a small, not very successful gift shop, and Fede was nearly penniless when I met him. He had free accommodation in someone's semi-finished basement, in return for menial work in the house. They did not provide him with a bed, and before we met he'd slept on blankets on the linoleum floor. I gave him a futon my mother had bought but never used.

He survived on student loans and a weekend job at a camera shop, which he loved. But Fede loved everything. We would walk for hours through unfamiliar parts of the city and every few minutes Fede would stop and exclaim in a way that was both theatrical and genuine: 'Oh look! Madness!' That was his word for things that captivated him: madness. Muslim children watching TV while doing homework at the back of a grocery store, a dusty Barbie astronaut in a shop window, an egg cup on a park bench—these anthropological tidbits stirred

his imagination, and he'd shriek with delight. He would
take out his camera, fiddle with it—this was before digital
cameras—and take a photo. Sometimes he asked me to
pose with the image, and I did, though always with my
back to the camera.

In some ways he was like Selena, but unlike her he was
spoiled, for his parents had adored and coddled him, and
he was a committed iconoclast when it came to conven-
tion and etiquette. Etiquette was 'madness' and he liked
to photograph it—he was always on the lookout for old
women who still wore gloves and a hat. But the idea of
imposed rules alarmed him, no matter how innocuous
they might seem to others.

I was happy—more than happy. In spite of my stain,
I was loved, I was having sex. My half-brother Owen
was in Taiwan for the year, and I was plant-sitting at his
Liberty Village condo suite, with its nine-foot ceilings,
track lighting, bad art, and a spectacular view of the city
against the sky. I cooked vegetarian feasts for my slight
lover, 'so you won't disappear altogether,' I'd tell him.
Then we'd put on Mozart's Requiem and in front of the
stainless steel fireplace we'd do the things lovers do.

For a few minutes, writing about Fede, I forgot that my
son is gone. When I finished writing—it must have been
a split-second but seemed longer—I remembered only

that something huge had happened in my life. Something dramatic.

My brain is pushing the death of my son to a new location. This is evolutionary, primal. The human race cannot allow its members to die of grief, or there will be no one left.

It's snowing today. The first snowfall my son will not see. Nor will he see Pursie crouching on her table in the back porch, enthralled by the large, swirling flakes and, after careful deliberation, swiping at them with an outstretched paw.

There will be hundreds, thousands of these firsts, from now on. I pulled out the Coleman sleeping bag I use as a quilt in winter. It's a deep orange-red, the colour of a Northern Cardinal. There are two in the linen chest—one for me, one for my son. He loved that sleeping bag, and said it made him look forward to winter.

Oh God, let me die of grief, let me be the exception!

If Neil has left Sherry, maybe he can take Pursie now. She's not afraid of dogs, and Ursula and Gudrun are the gentlest of creatures—they were mistreated by their former owner and have become inordinately attached to Neil. They express their gratitude by trying to anticipate his every wish. If he wanted them to be protective of a cat, they would guard her with their lives.

Women don't steal men. Humans don't romantically steal other humans. We go where we want to go.

A woman at a party set her eyes on Fede, and her heart, and whatever other body part she could rally for Operation Get Fede.

Kim, her name was. She was charming and alluring and she wore magnificent clothes, convincingly just-put-together-from-odds-and-ends. She was in my program, though her passion was fashion, as she liked to say. I remember, at the party, sensing her interest in Fede. Then she ate a mille feuille and licked her sticky fingers, one by one. I saw Fede looking at her, and I knew at that moment, from the way he was watching her, that they'd either had sex already or were about to.

I didn't think she was Fede's type, I thought it would be a passing whim, but I was wrong. He fell in love with her and left me. Such simple words, such a simple event.

Heartbreak is different from real loss. I knew that even back then. The lover's betrayal detracts from his appeal, and anger and disgust take over. I cried for weeks, felt like crying for months, but I knew I'd get over it, and I did.

Had I really thought a man could love me? My father was right, after all. For though he was never explicit about it, it was more than obvious that my father didn't trust Fede. He thought Fede was too tiny to be attractive to normal women, and was with me only for the sex.

It occurs to me that my father never understood one single thing about our gender. He couldn't see how enticing Fede was to women, how lovely his slim, lithe body was, and everything else about him—his playful eyes, his contented smile, his dusky olive skin. I have to remember that my father, who was born in 1911, hailed from a different eon as far as the male–female thing went. He never really adjusted his antiquated views, though he hid them when necessary.

I didn't tell my parents what had happened. I stopped mentioning Fede and they never asked about him. It was easy to hide my heartbreak, for we were all busy, and months went by without more than a perfunctory phone call.

And so Fede vanished from my life. I don't know whether he became a photojournalist, whether he's married now, whether he has children. Every now and then I'd Google him, just out of curiosity, but his last name, Garza, was common, and so was his first, if he now went by Federico.

A satisfying snowstorm outside. I hope it rips the city apart. I hope roofs fly off houses, I hope windows shatter. But no, maybe not—because *what will the robin do then, poor thing?*

Pursie is afraid of the howling wind. She hides under anything snuggly—pillows, blankets. Or my son's windbreaker, which is still here on the sofa, a ghostly embodiment of his absence. I can't bear that it's here, can't bear to move it. Where would I move it to? I hug the windbreaker as I watch whatever is on my screen. I've been borrowing DVDs by the carload. The library has a large collection, thanks to revenue from fines and a package deal with British television—hundreds of hours, if you add them up. And since I replay the DVDs over and over—I can watch the same thing for a week and not take anything in, really—it comes to thousands.

I am unable to relate to the quality or content of these productions. Instead, I find myself mesmerized by the print on a character's dress, or the emotions crossing a face, or the way the furniture is arranged in a room. But the story, the words—that part fails to reach the sorting channels of my brain. I don't know what's going on, don't want to know.

During our ten months together, Neil and I found great pleasure—or at least I did—in watching films together. It seemed miraculous, how we always laughed at the same things for the same reason, got bored or disgusted for the same reason, wept for the same reason. 'It's as if we were brother and sister in another life,' Neil said.

I wonder, did Neil know I was home that Wednesday, eleven years ago, when he said those things to Dominic? Neil—the most intuitive person I've come across, the person who always divined what our son wanted, long before he could speak or point.

It never occurred to me that he might have wanted me

to hear his confession, but I'm slow. It takes me years to work out all sorts of things a sharper person would see right away—sneaky or devious things, mostly.

Maybe Neil was looking for a way out, a way to tell me he wanted out. And that was how he chose to do it. He chose to have me listen in on his stoned conversation.

If I asked him now, he'd be honest with me, but I no longer care.

The owner of the white car assaulted me today at the supermarket, in the vegetable section.

He followed me from my house. I think he's been following me for a long time, but I never look at anyone.

This time he came over and said my name. I turned, and his face filled me with undefined horror, as if I'd seen a devil, or worse. I didn't know who he was, only that I wanted to shrink away from him, or else slash a knife through his heart.

Instead I picked up a cauliflower. That was what came to hand. I picked it up and threatened him with it.

Then I realized who it was. It was the man who killed my son.

He said he needed to talk to me, he had something to tell me, something important.

Something important—to whom? Not to me, that much was certain. The only important thing he could have to tell me was that my son was actually alive because there had been a mistake at the hospital—he was alive but in a coma and might still wake up. I've actually had that fantasy, and one night I even called the hospital to make sure.

I began to run away from him, pushing my cart in front of me. He shouted after me, 'I was on Demerol, I don't know why it didn't show up! I was on Demerol!'

I flew through the oversized swinging doors marked EMPLOYEES ONLY and found myself in a dank cement warehouse, amidst towering piles of cardboard boxes and industrial trolleys. Two male workers in green aprons looked at me in alarm.

'There's a man following me,' I said, aware that I came across as delusional. But then a motherly woman, sweaty and breathless in her flowered dress, poked her head through the door.

'Poor dear,' she said. 'What a dreadful thing! Dreadful!'

The supermarket workers were visibly relieved. They immediately strode out, manly and affronted, to see what they could do, but the child psychiatrist had vanished.

Not enough that he killed my son, he wants something from me!

What does that mean, that he was on Demerol? What does it mean? My head is spinning.

I've been out on the road today, to see what the child psychiatrist would have seen. Back and forth I drove, back and forth, in barely controlled fury.

The road is completely flat where we live. He would have spotted my son from way off.

He wanted to kill him. Some part of him wanted to kill a child. If he hadn't wanted to kill a child, he would have stayed awake at least until he passed the boy crouching in the grass.

He came to me to confess that he'd been on drugs. Why confess to me? I'm not the police.

Somehow the blood test was flawed, or else the lab technician lost or dropped the sample and invented results—who knows? Paul Bernardo's blood tests were ignored for two years—two years during which he could have been behind bars instead of on killing sprees. A technical oversight.

My mother, who was good at her job but had to deal with a multitude of other professionals, used to say, 'Isn't it amazing how many people are bad at what they do?' She'd say, 'Hairdressers, doctors, flower arrangers—it makes no difference. Half or more are incompetent.' It was her favourite mantra, recited continually as she scurried about, planning her latest event.

Hairdressers and lab technicians and also child psychiatrists who hate children and secretly want to kill them and then do kill them, who drive on Demerol and then weeks later come chasing after their victims, whose lives they have destroyed, with the effrontery to ask for—what?

Am I supposed to call the police now? Send them to his house, so they can hear his confession and retry him? He'll deny it all—why would he want to go to jail? He is playing evil mind games with me.

If he dares to show up here again in his new white car, I'll get a restraining order. Was it unpleasant, Mr. Waste-of-Space Psychiatrist, driving the burgundy car, with those bloodstains on the fenders? Yes, bury it all, get a new car, get on with your miserable life, you miserable piece of slime.

But what good does all this anger do? It wears me out with its futility and stupidity.

Ever since the incident at the supermarket I've been having afternoon nightmares, the kind I had that first day, before the drugs arrived. The child psychiatrist gouged open a cavern leading straight to hell, and let loose a new demon, one that is immune to chemical manipulation.

I'll be lying on the sofa, watching something or other, and without warning my eyelids grow heavier, until I can no longer raise them. I want to sit up and shake off the drowsiness, but my body refuses to budge. And then the front of the car that killed my son, huge and metal and menacing, comes speeding at me like a giant killing machine, but it's my son who collapses under it. The same thing, again and again, I can't stop the replay. I want to scream, because a scream would wake me, but I have no voice. And the radio, the radio that won't stop playing though I try to stomp on it with my heavy work boots—it's playing 'Swing Low, Sweet Chariot,' or is it 'Strange Fruit,' but the sound is distorted and terrifying.

And then the bloated animal corpses again ...

I need stronger drugs. I'm also running low on the venom-green pills. I have to get a refill, but I keep putting it off.

In the past, it was my stain that made a trip to the corner store an ordeal. My first stain-related memory is of rain. I was visiting my grandparents at their country house, and since my grandmother and I were the only ones who rose at dawn, the two of us would set off for an early morning walk in the forest, along a well-kept path. The walk was an enormous treat. We wore black rain boots and looked out for white-tailed deer. The deer were accustomed to humans, some of whom fed them, and rarely bothered to flee. They preferred to stand, motionless, and gaze at us. The adult deer were better at not moving than their offspring, who were still learning the skill.

That morning was particularly misty, and it soon began to drizzle. My grandmother said, 'The mist and rain make everything beautiful.' I was puzzled, because the forest was beautiful as it was, and decided she was referring not only to the forest, but to the entire world. I stopped walking and lifted my face to the rain. My grandmother asked me what I was doing and I told her I was waiting for the rain to make me beautiful. I didn't mean it literally—it was merely a fantasy, a flight of the imagination. I had been told that my birthmark was permanent.

My grandmother was very upset. 'You're beautiful as you are,' she scolded. 'And don't let anyone tell you otherwise. Anyone who can't see that is blind.'

I think now that she was angry at my mother. It must have been a bone of contention between them, my mother's distress at my disfigurement. *Disfigurement*— that's my mother's word, or would be. But in fact my stain is nothing more than a human variation.

Really it's not very complicated. My mother's life revolved around décor. It was her profession and obsession: creating the perfect setting, ensuring that every detail was coordinated—flowers, attire, tableware. She used screens to hide a room's less presentable features, fretted over dusty windows and dreary floors. As for her own appearance, she felt it had to inspire confidence in her clients. Who would hire an event planner with chipped nail polish?

I did not inherit the curse of pointless perfectionism, but my fine arts teachers did complain that my work was too pretty. They'd shake their heads and say, 'Very good, but too pretty.'

As in the old days, I have to steel myself when I go out, but the pitfalls have changed. I am no longer self-conscious, no longer afraid of stares. Overnight that pack of nonsense was dismantled, overnight it disintegrated into nothing. What a flailing at windmills!

Now the dangers do not reside in any one place or event. They hover in the air like invisible needles and my body tenses with unnamed dread. It is the only time I long for a companion: someone who will do the talking for me, hold me up if I become unhinged. An imaginary person who requires nothing from me, not even acknowledgement.

I change my shirt, braid my hair. Armed with sunglasses, I step outside. The light and air are like treacherous sirens, deceiving me. I make my way to the car and hope that I remember how to drive standard.

I do remember, miraculously. The drive to the new shopping centre at the edge of town takes only a few minutes. I park at the far corner, and enter the pharmacy's vast, brightly lit cosmetics section—my mother's territory but as foreign to me as a space station. How can there be so many products for the adornment of a single human face, a single body?

I'm always greeted with forced chirpiness by the woman who sits, bored out of her mind, behind the futuristic-white makeup counter. Calling out a greeting is part of her job, and she must hate it as much as the customers do. I pretend to be deaf.

I don't need to say much at the prescription booth. Only one of the pharmacists is easy to deal with. The others are arrogant or dour, or both. The worst of the lot is a handsome Sri Lankan who seems to think he is a god among men. We vaguely hate each other, but our exchange is brief. I hand him my health card and he refills my prescription.

The Sri Lankan announced this morning that my refill has expired.

I was seized with fear and began to back away. In surprising, uncharacteristic confusion, he said, 'Just phone your doctor.'

Then he asked, 'Are you all right?' His face was transformed in that instant and I saw another side of him, a side that was decent and even a little bashful.

I nodded and turned away, wondering where I could find a payphone. Did they still exist, outside of airports? I couldn't think straight.

I sat in my car until eventually an image pushed its way through the panic: the mall has public phones.

I turned on the ignition and, trying not to think, I set out. A distant part of my brain, one that had nothing to do with me, knew the way.

We had strolled through the town's mall a thousand times, my son and I. We looked for things we needed and bought french fries at the food court. My son liked to browse through the bookstore and electronics shop. Sometimes we couldn't find what we wanted and we'd go from store to store until suddenly at the exact same moment we'd both get mallitis and I'd have an attack of uncontrollable giggles as we made our getaway. 'Hurry,' I'd say, choking on my laughter, 'before they activate the alien implants!'

I didn't want to enter the mall without my son. I began to tremble. There has to be meaning to things. If there's no meaning, then where are you? If there's no meaning, you're in freefall, with nothing to hold onto.

Yet I had no choice. *Huit clos*. All exits closed.

At least I didn't have to go far—the phone stall is right near the entrance. I leaned on the curved partition to steady myself, and by mistake dialled 911 instead of the directory, 411.

'This is 911,' the operator said furiously, when I asked for the number of the clinic, and he hung up in disgust as I began stuttering my apology.

I didn't give myself a chance to fall apart. I quickly dialled 411 and was asked whether I wanted to be connected to the clinic. The small, unexpected service— I thought I'd have to make a separate call—helped to counteract the 911 bungle.

The receptionist at the clinic asked me to hold while

she checked my file. When she came back on the line, her voice had changed. She now spoke in the guarded tone of someone who's seen the test results and knows what's coming but isn't allowed to say. Except that in my case it had already come. She told me the doctor needed to see me in person—could I come in today? Dr. Stuart had a spot at four.

But I need a day to get ready. My appointment is for tomorrow at half past three.

Maybe it's just as well—I'll ask Dr. Stuart for something stronger, something that can outwit the nightmare demon.

But what if she refuses to give me anything?

Maybe asking for something stronger will work against me. Should I tell her about my other ailments? Stomach pain and digestive problems. Nausea. Headaches. A type of shortness of breath that's hard to describe—as if I can't fill my lungs. Numb, tingling limbs. Shivers. Burning eyes. Pain in my wrists. Pain everywhere.

Will a catalogue of these symptoms make my case stronger or weaken it? I don't know what to do.

I told Dr. Stuart about the child psychiatrist.

I didn't plan to do it, but that was the first thing I said.

She asked, 'How have you been managing?' and I said, 'The man who was driving—you know, the car—he told me he was on Demerol.'

Though I hadn't been aware of it, I must have been waiting for an opportunity to unload the burden that had been dumped on me like a shower of nuclear fallout. Under the weight of the one thing I want, and can't have, my whole wanting mechanism has broken down.

And I'd forgotten the aura of competence and intelligence that fills the room when Dr. Stuart enters it. She forces herself to be professional, she works at it, because she's so young and pretty and approachable that her patients must all want to rest their heads on her pillowy bosom.

My words shocked her, though she did her best not to show it. 'Did he write to you?' she asked.

I described the scene at the supermarket. She pursed her lips and said, 'Leave it with me.' And that was that. The monkey was off my back.

I told her about the nightmares and she began to enumerate the advantages and drawbacks of each drug and how they might or might not behave or interact with one another. I nodded my head as if it all made sense, but I wasn't able to concentrate on anything she said. And since I couldn't follow, I couldn't make any decisions. It seems, therefore, that I am stuck for now with the venom-green capsules, the chalk-blue sleeping pills, and the daytime descent into hell.

When that was settled, or not settled, she took my blood pressure and asked me to step on the scale. She was concerned that I'd lost so much weight. Was I eating?

I described my digestive problems and she prescribed something or other—I didn't keep the prescription. Then she asked whether there was anything else I wanted to tell her about. I shook my head. There wasn't any point going through my list of irrelevant symptoms. I was worn out and impatient to go home.

'Have you been in touch with the Bereavement Centre?' she asked.

I nodded—dishonestly, because that's not what she meant—and she nodded in return, and said she was very sorry for my loss. Tears filled her large dark eyes.

I didn't want to cry at the clinic. I rose from the seat, thanked her, stumbled down the stairs, and lurched to my car as if I were drunk. It's warm again, after the false start of winter last week, and the sun was out. Everything was very still. The small parking lot faces a modern facility of some kind, probably a nursing home or seniors' residence, and there's nothing but vacant land and trees on either side. I was free to hide my face on the steering wheel and sob.

That was my day. Somehow I survived. I survived standing in line in the waiting room, approaching the receptionist, being called in, talking to Dr. Stuart. Yet it all seemed hazy, as if I were underwater, and could only see and hear indistinctly.

I had been terrified that Dr. Stuart might say something that would hurt me and dishonour my son and diminish his death, but she didn't. I almost wrote, just now, that I was lucky—but I will never be able to use that word, *lucky*, again. *Lucky* and also *grateful*. Those words are no longer part of any language I know.

But Dr. Stuart's tact and her help with the child psychiatrist were a relief, yes.

Pursie has escaped! I went to put out the garbage and I must have absent-mindedly failed to click the door shut, and she pushed against it and crept out while my back was turned.

I've been looking for her everywhere, calling out her name frantically—but it's dark now and I can't see anything. There are very few cars on this semi-rural road at night—almost none—but I think I will go out and sit on the road anyhow, just in case. I hear my son's voice: *Mom, how could you, how could you?*

The little imp! I sat on the road for hours, shivering and calling out her name, and when I went inside to pee, there she was, sitting calmly in front of the door so that I nearly tripped over her.

I grabbed her and brought her in. Her paws were muddy—the snow that fell last week melted with the rising temperatures and left everything sodden. She knew she'd have a hard time cleaning the mud off herself, and she allowed me to wipe her paws with a washcloth. That is, she instinctively pulled each paw back as I wiped it, but didn't try to get away. She seemed pleased with the adventure she'd had, and seemed also to know that she'd worried me.

She settled herself next to me on the sofa and placed her paw on my arm. It's something she likes to do—place one or both front paws on a human leg or arm. My son adored that about her, and more than once I came into his room to find him sleeping with his palm out and Pursie's paw resting in it.

I'm wondering now whether I should let her out on a long leash and sit and watch her, at least for a little while each day. Or maybe I could build a fence out back—a very tall one, made of smooth aluminum that doesn't provide any purchase, and she could wander freely within the enclosure. Anyhow, I can't imagine her trying to climb a fence. She can barely manoeuvre herself from the floor to the sofa.

There might be just enough time to put up a fence before the ground freezes again. I could hire Donald, the odd-job man, to build it. His card is on the fridge door, held in place by a dancing-frog magnet that caught my son's eye during a road trip to Vermont. He was eight, and we'd stopped for homemade peach ice cream at a crafts store. He laughed when he saw the magnet, a frog that jiggles when you touch it, and he went on laughing at it the entire day. I was delighted that something so small could make him so happy. That's the way it is with children, if all is well.

I will have to open an email account, but it will be for Donald only. No one else will know about it.

My new email address is as impersonal as I can make it: *needcatfence@yahoo.com*. I've become an expert at avoidance in this landmine-strewn world.

I asked Donald whether he and two or three friends would be available to build a fence. I offered him $10,000 plus the cost of materials. Exorbitant, I suppose, but I have no need of money, none at all. What I do need is a fence. And Donald can use the money.

He answered immediately. He thought I'd made a mistake in the price, but I explained that I wanted a very tall, very long fence and I needed it right away. I sent him an echeque for $3,000 for supplies.

The fence could enclose my shed. It could be a fence for me too: I'll be able to sit inside the fenced-in area in the spring and no one will be able to look in. No one will be able to catch me unawares. We will expand our cloister, Pursie and I.

Donald did some research and sent me a long, detailed letter about types of fences. I didn't read it.

I wrote back:

> Hi Donald, Please do whatever you think best.
> The only requirements are that it's snug on the
> ground so the cat can't slip under it, and at
> least eight feet high. Any material a cat would
> have difficulty scaling is fine. Also something
> that provides complete privacy, so no one
> can see in, and whatever is fastest because it
> could get too cold or too wet any day now. I
> don't care about appearance. And I don't care
> about the cost, so just buy whatever you think
> will work. Also the bird bath will have to be
> moved. It might be easier to cover it and get a
> new bird bath and feeder, the heated type, for
> the front of the house—please install it under
> the large oak. I appreciate your help.

How money galvanizes people—the pickup truck arrived at nine this morning, and Donald and two of his friends jumped out, their faces brimming with amiability. They seem ready to love me for my generosity, as they see it. It's not generosity, it's selfishness, really, but they can't see that.

I realized that Donald didn't know about my son. I prayed he wouldn't ask—I decided that if he did, I would be evasive. I'd say only, 'He's not here.' But so far he hasn't asked.

There is much activity outdoors: mowing, drilling, digging, hammering. In the past I would have joined in. In the past I liked do-it-yourself. I discovered its pleasures when I took a course in set design at university, and we created a complex structure for a Chekhov play: sliding panels, receding corridors, a magical rotating forest.

That sort of excitement has been ripped out of me. Everything inside me was tied to my son. All that's left now is skin, bones, cartilage. Cells doing their thing.

I stand in the back porch and look out at the strong bodies, so full of vitality and a kind of grace—even the short, chubby guy with the mermaid tattoo. The grace of being alive.

Suddenly I say, 'Look, darling. Look at the fence they're making for Pursie. I wonder why we didn't think of it before.' And for several seconds I manage to believe that he's there.

⬥

I drew and painted my son throughout his life, and the walls of the house are covered with these framed declarations of love. He took it all in stride, as if it were my business, not his. And he was right, of course. It was all about my feelings, and also my creative efforts.

When he was young he constantly commissioned me. It made me laugh, the way he'd bring me a blank piece of paper and issue his peremptory order. *Draw a giant armadillo. Draw a wildebeest.* He was such a polite boy, always saying please and thank you and could I, but when it came to these requisitions, he was dictatorial—or rather, princely, as if he were merely collecting what was his due. I think it was the intensity of his need that he was trying to disguise.

I was eventually usurped by various computer programs Neil installed for him. The drawings I made for my son, along with most of my attempts to capture his spirit on paper and canvas, are in storage bins in the basement. His schoolwork and swimming certificates and old toys are there too. Photographs are mostly stored in files in my computer. I open these files compulsively throughout the day.

How can the torments of the damned be at the same time angelic gifts? How is that possible? I don't mean suffering dressed up as glory—I mean photographs that slam into me like an avalanche of burning rocks, and also reach out to me tenderly.

I've been to Scotiabank to take out ten thousand dollars—
ten packets of ten one-hundred-dollar bills.

I've managed to avoid going to the bank until now. The
only familiar strangers I've been forced to interact with
are librarians, when I check out my DVDs. They knew
us well at the library, because of Neil's afternoon visits
with our son, and my frequent borrowing. A welcoming
library—not large but built with careful attention to
comfort. Sofas, magazines, polished oak tables, and the
sun streaming in through translucent blinds.

Now I wear sunglasses and keep my face averted
from the gaze of the librarians. They understand, and
say nothing. I can tell they feel bad for me. Only the
temporary workers, who don't know me, say, chillingly,
'Have a nice day.'

I wanted to be anonymous at the bank, but there
were only two tellers serving customers, and both recognized me instantly. I chose the older one, Judith, whose
sculpted model's face has gently softened with age. She
once mentioned, when the subject of the Hillside Music
Festival came up, that she sings scat.

As soon as she saw me, her face registered distress.
She's not allowed to say anything, and I think she was
relieved, because what is there to say?

I told her I needed to withdraw ten thousand dollars.
She lowered her voice and said confidentially that usually
the bank asks for two days' notice when it's such a large
amount, and also I have to let them know what it's for.

'A fence,' I muttered and, as if echoing me, she coached, 'Renovations?' and I nodded. It took a long time and I had to sign many forms—it seems the bank has instructions to track the circulation of large amounts of cash. They were able in the end to make an exception for me, and they gave me the money on the spot.

I did all right. I don't know what's worse, feeling deranged or doing all right. For there's something ruthless about doing all right. It feels like desertion, as if, for half an hour, I had turned my back on my poor little son, my little boy.

***

The fence is complete. The guys came today to add reinforcements, install the new bird bath, and add a cat flap to the porch door. They were very moved yesterday when I paid them the entire amount, even though there was still more to do. The reverence in their eyes as I handed them the bills was astounding to me—all because I'd paid them more than the going rate.

Donald noticed that the eavestrough needed cleaning and, without asking, he set his ladder against the roof, removed the old sponge filters and swept away the leaves. When he'd finished, he sent one of his friends to buy new filters. All day he puttered around, looking for things to fix and adjust. As if he knew, somehow, that I wasn't up to the usual maintenance.

The fence is made of beige aluminum siding and does not include a gate. The only way to enter the enclosure is through the porch. I wanted to let Pursie out into her new yard right away, but she was frightened when I opened the porch door, and peered out from a safe distance.

I waited for a while, then came inside and made coffee. I left the back door open, and the house grew cold, but I forgot to put on my coat.

Pursie finally stepped outdoors. I watched her through the screen window as she roamed and explored and investigated. She was particularly interested in the shed, and I wondered whether she could smell the horses that were once sheltered there. As I'd predicted, she made no attempt to scale the fence. She accepts whatever fate imposes on her, including aluminum walls. It wouldn't occur to her to try trickery or cook up schemes.

Her evident enjoyment as she sniffed the weeds should have given me a sense of satisfaction, or at least accomplishment, but instead, as I followed her careful movements with my eyes, a new type of sadness, as heavy and deep as molten lead, came seeping through me.

Maybe it was seeing those men at work. Every day I think of my son's lost future, the future that will never be. Middle school, high school, swimming team meets. Dating, college, learning to drive. Being a man, with a man's responsibilities. A trip to Europe with friends, backpacking in the wilderness. Love, children, work. Our future has been stolen away.

I am lonely, indescribably lonely, for this future.

⸺

Well, at least Christmas never meant anything to me. I'm half-Jewish, though not in the usual way. Both my parents had one Jewish parent: my mother's mother, my father's mother.

But that's not the reason. My father was always away at Christmas, seeing his other families, and my mother, to compensate, would take me somewhere warm for the week, usually with a friend of hers. Cuba, Florida, New Orleans—they're all a blur, those winter holidays. Crowded airports, delayed flights, swimming pools. My mother and whatever friend she'd brought along—usually someone she worked with—doing laps and discussing food while I read moodily under a parasol. I didn't know how to swim and didn't want to learn. I must have been an uncompanionable companion.

And Neil hated Christmas, for reasons unknown. We celebrated the winter solstice with our son, which fizzled inevitably into nothing but a meal with presents.

Still, Christmas is quieter now, emptier, I don't know why. Maybe it's the intuition that elsewhere families are celebrating. The air must be filled with celebration atoms, and those of us who stand barefoot in the snow, looking in through the window, wanting what we cannot have— we know ourselves to be outcasts. My son was a link to holidays and festivals and merrymaking. For he loved all those things, and led us to them.

There is not much point to all this lamenting. It's over, and that's all there is to it.

How to go on. Hamlet's question, and mine. He feared damnation, and I cannot abandon Pursie. Though what Hamlet, or anyone who has not lost a child, really has to complain about I don't know.

It occurs to me that I must make provisions for Pursie, in case of my death. For though we have no full-length mirrors in the house, I know I am shrinking. My jeans are loose on me, and I've had to take in my sweatpants. I woke up this morning with a cold. If I don't look after myself it will turn into bronchitis or pneumonia. My body may simply give up on me.

There's Neil, but I have no way of discovering whether he's left Sherry. Even if I were to look through her Facebook postings—which would mean opening my son's computer—they would not reveal anything, for she never mentioned Neil to her contacts. She wants to keep the secret treasure all to herself.

Do I even trust Neil? Not that he'd ever harm an

animal, but how can I trust someone who let Sherry and her pitiful children into his life? If he didn't protect his son, would he protect Pursie?

No, I must find someone who would be willing to move in here. I'd leave them the house and all I have, on condition that they look after Pursie.

What about Selena? Maybe I can find her.

As a matter of fact, I think I hate Neil.

I mean, damn him to hell for what he did to our son, for the garbage—literally—he dumped him into. It's not Sherry's fault—it has nothing to do with her. It's him. It's what he did.

Damn him to hell.

The days lumber on. The heaviness that descended on me when the fence was completed has replaced the nightmares. Winter has officially arrived, and darkness with it. I lie under the Coleman sleeping bag and pray for unconsciousness. Internet research led me to melatonin, the one substance I can mix with my drugs and find on a supermarket shelf. With the combined assistance of the chalk-blue pill and the melatonin, I manage to sleep twelve or even thirteen hours a day, but the remaining hours stretch out before me like enemy territory, or no man's land, which must be somehow traversed.

I can no longer watch DVDs. I lie on the sofa and listen to Mozart's Requiem, over and over, all day long. Was it bad luck to play the Requiem at Owen's place, during sex with Fede? It's the only music that makes sense now. How pretentious we were—or maybe just innocent. I didn't hear the fury and despair in the music then. It didn't occur to me, because I couldn't have known, that the Dies Irae has nothing to do with God's judgment, but with ours. It is we who pour out our wrath and incredulity. There is no reconciliation, no peace, no acceptance—only different modes of sorrow, including weariness.

On the morning my son died, I was eating some dates from a small transparent container. He picked one out, bit into it, then handed it back to me. 'Do you want this?' he asked. 'There's something wrong with it. It's too hard.'

I burst into laughter. 'What are you offering me? A half-eaten date that has something wrong with it?' I couldn't stop laughing, and he smiled, used to my outbursts and glad to see me amused. Nothing makes children happier than seeing their parents laugh.

We had such a fine life. Why him? Why?

My son's birthday. I baked a birthday cake, I lit candles, I blew them out. It was an act of masochism, I think now, yet not baking a cake would have been no better.

I don't understand anything. I don't understand why I'm here, staring at a birthdayless birthday cake—it's as if the cake were in the wrong painting, the one with a tombstone instead of a party.

I don't understand why my son isn't here. I don't understand why the life of someone like my son was extinguished.

We always made a big fuss over our son's birthday. The day before the party I'd decorate the house, and then Neil would come over and we'd have a pre-birthday supper, the three of us, as if we were still living together. My son got upset if we gave him too many presents, so we controlled ourselves. He was always like that—even when he was three he didn't like having a surplus of toys. He wanted to get to know his toys, he said, which meant not being inundated. One Saturday, when he was in grade one or two, he played for ten hours straight with his plastic dinosaurs. I brought him his meals on the floor because he didn't want to interrupt his game. He was so quiet that I kept peeking into his room to see if he was all right.

He did not deserve this death.

january

I woke up in the middle of the night, sweating and feverish, with Pursie perched heavily on my chest. My sleep had been broken and vexed, the sort you have when you're ill, but the chalk-blue pill must have kept me from waking until Pursie settled on me.

She was purring her airplane-engine purr, pushing her small head against my throat, licking my chin with her rough tongue. When she first came to live with us, we were surprised and charmed by how frequently she licked us, and my son, wondering what was behind it, researched the subject. He was pleased to discover that Pursie's enthusiastic licks conveyed not only a predilection for the taste of skin, but also affection and hopefulness, a request not to be left or given away.

I turned over, dislodging her, but she installed herself beside me, her warm body pressing lightly against my back. I was so close, so close to drifting away from a life I can't sustain. Another day might have done it. And here she was, all ego and selfishness, refusing to be left. 'Narcissist,' I accused her.

My body ached, and with each cough white pain flared through my chest. I pulled myself out of bed, turned up the heat in the house, made myself tea, searched the drawers and cupboards for acetaminophen. I found the bottle among the spices, swallowed three regular-strength pills, and tried to remember what I'd done with Dr. Stuart's prescription, the one for stomach problems.

Did I really need my winter coat, for a sprint to the car? Such a temptation, not to put it on. 'Oh, have it your way,' I grumbled at Pursie. Bundled in the zipped-up coat and, for the first time this winter, my wool pilot hat, I made my way to the car. It's been snowing heavily these past two days, and I noticed that Lloyd, the semi-retired snowplough guy with whom I have an annual contract, had cleared the drive. He has a copy of the car key and usually comes while I'm asleep. He moves my neolithic vehicle out of the way and, after he's ploughed the long driveway, returns it to its place. Lloyd—such a gentleman he is. A breed that won't exist in a few years.

I switched on the interior light and there it was, the prescription, on the car floor, crumpled up but otherwise intact. My arm banged against the glove compartment as I reached over, and it flew open. My son used to complain that the glove compartment slammed down on his knees. I suggested he move the seat back, but he liked to be close to the windshield, he said. He got stuck sometimes, my son. He couldn't solve his problem because the solution entailed a different drawback. It exasperated me at times, though at other times I was amused and teased him. 'Guess you're stuck between the snowman and the rain, sweetheart,' I'd say.

My fever made me light-headed. I stayed up, waiting for the pharmacy to open. I drank tea and stroked Pursie and took more pills. A blurred grey dawn crawled in. Dark became murky, murky became dim. I drove to the pharmacy and bought what turned out to be chewable tablets and a liquid medicine. Both are suitably disgusting.

I made myself a pot of rice with whatever vegetables had not gone bad in the fridge. I added a tablespoon of olive oil to the rice, and some of my spice mix. I haven't touched the spice mix, which I make—made—in a coffee grinder, since my son died. He loved that mix and put it on everything.

When the rice was ready, I forced myself to eat the entire potful.

Happy, Pursie?

Out of sheer boredom I'm going to try the Bereavement Centre. I've lost all discernment anyhow, so won't know if it doesn't go well. I'm only half here, or rather one thousandth here.

I found the bereavement woman's card, and gave her name when I called. I didn't want to be questioned, and I assumed that if I mentioned her visit I'd bypass having to say the words, 'my son died'—which would not have been possible. My strategy worked. The receptionist, who was doing her best to sound sympathetic, didn't ask any questions. She said a volunteer counsellor will call me, and in the meantime I can come to the Morning Retreat, a program they run three times a week.

Also, I'm on antibiotics. I went to the after-hours clinic and saw a nameless, faceless doctor. He listened to my chest and scribbled something down. I was laconic, he was laconic. It took all of five minutes.

Oh, paltry, paltry!

At first I was incensed, offended, scandalized. I could hardly believe that such paltry—such kitschy—wares were on offer. It was exactly what I'd feared, and worse. I wanted to tear my hair out.

But then, all at once, a huge wave of pity swept away my dismay. I thought of an impoverished village my father had been to, on one of his pipe-installation missions. He brought back a photo of merchandise that had been set on a table in the centre of the village. What sad, little items were lined up there! Two pencils, a comb, shoe-laces, cloth pouches, empty jars, a tiny doll ... it broke my heart. The obscene, mindless surfeit of things here—the world made no sense.

It was the same at the Bereavement Centre. The antagonism I felt when I saw the slogans printed on flyers—slogans involving doors and rainbows and stairs—for a few minutes I didn't know what to do with myself. But in a flash it came to me: *this is all there is.* These measly wares are all anyone can offer. Death is all-powerful, and we have only a comb, a few shoelaces, to counter it. I felt pity for the Bereavement Centre, for everyone in it, for all of us.

I let myself lose my personality in their kindness. The receptionist gave me a hug. How long since I've been hugged? There were only old women there, grieving the loss of husbands. I wondered whether people like me, for whom there is no hope of solace, stay away—we are too fragile, too weepy, for tai chi and therapeutic touch. Yet I did it all. A tai chi video from my twenties came back to me as I followed the steps of a brightly dressed Australian instructor. A volunteer named Marmie—isn't that from *Little Women?*—gently touched me as I lay on a chaise longue with my eyes shut. How long since someone touched my wrists? Not since Fede.

They give massages, too, but you have to book in advance. I asked for an appointment and they put me down for next week.

It's the venom-green pills, of course, that make it possible for me to suspend disbelief.

This state of suspension—it's a form of somnambu-
lism. I am half-asleep, half-awake. This must be what
it's like to sink into senility. The present merges with the
past because everything you do is distant, a re-enactment
of something imperfectly remembered. I am an actor in
someone's dream play.

Someone dreamt my visit to the Bereavement Centre,
someone dreamt the brightly dressed Australian and the
meditation circle and especially Marmie, who laid her
hands lovingly on my shoulders, my hands, my feet, in an
effort to help me overcome the loss of my son.

I've been trying to find Selena. Googling 'Selena Blanco'
didn't get me anywhere, and it seems there's a famous
football player called Sebastian Blanco. I created a fake
Facebook page and searched for her there, but there were
dozens of women with her name. Of course she may
not be on Facebook, or she may have set her page to
unsearchable.

But I can't think of any other way to track her down,
if this doesn't work. In the old days you could put an ad
in the classifieds of a newspaper, but now everything is
online, and all I found there was a helter-skelter of search
wars.

I began sifting through the Facebook list, but soon
grew discouraged. What am I looking for? Who knows

whether Selena is alive, even, or how she's changed over the years.

And what exactly do I want of her? What are the odds that she is in a position to look after a cat?

Apart from all that, how can I ask a favour of someone when I have nothing to offer? Jealousy, in spite of my stain, was dormant in me most of my life—I don't know why. Even when Fede left me, jealousy played only a small part in my heartbreak. Maybe seeing the corrosive effects of jealousy on my father distanced me from the emotion.

Whatever the reason, I have changed drastically. I am jealous now even of fictional characters in sitcoms. I seethe with jealousy every time I see a child. And when a mother at the supermarket behaves with dim-witted, damaging callousness towards her child, I want to kick her until she's unconscious. I never knew I had such aggression in me.

This does not bode well for any sort of contact, even with Selena—or especially with Selena, who deserves better than this desiccated husk of a self.

The counsellor showed up today. What a fiasco!

I thought, somehow, that the bereavement woman would come, but it seems she's attached to the hospital and mostly works there.

The counsellor they sent me is not really a counsellor at all. She's a volunteer who gives her time and speaks from experience.

She's a tiny woman, but hard to miss. She was decked in peacock-feather earrings, bright green slacks, and a Winnie-the-Pooh sweater. It came to me that she was still dressing for her daughter, who died at age four, after a long illness. That's what she said: 'a long illness.' Most of what she said was borrowed from somewhere. She had lost the ability to come up with her own words. Maybe she was afraid of what her own words might be, and where they'd take her. Nowhere good.

She has three teenaged children and a husband. A loving husband, she said. Her daughter died nine years ago. Her daughter's spirit is with her always. Her daughter blessed her with her death. Her daughter's death bestowed gifts upon her. The volunteer's voice was as frail as her tiny body.

I was dumbfounded, listening to her. Nine years, and three thriving children, and a husband—and here she is, clinging to the frayed heaving-lines flung to her from the cliché lifeboat, trying to buoy herself up on them. My heart ached for her. She had watched her tiny child suffer—who knew from what terrible disease—and had been unable to do anything. It had been too much to bear, and this was how she kept herself from going under.

Such last resorts are useless to me. How terrifying,

if this is all there is. No balm in Gilead, it seems, or anywhere else.

—————

Well, what about a real counsellor—a therapist?

My mother took me to a therapist once, when I was in high school. It upset her that I refused invitations to parties and locked myself in my room, reading and drawing and studying for exams.

An odd reason to worry, but in fact my mother was not so much worried as hampered by pesky guilt. She blamed herself for my reclusiveness, for when I was younger, she wouldn't let me enter event rooms, even before people arrived, because she was afraid I'd ruin the *mise en scène* she'd worked so hard to create. She might as well have been born in some benighted era of the past, my mother, when imperfect children were hidden away in attics.

But it wasn't only me. She refused to hire caterers whose waiters were untidy or had bad skin. She tried to talk brides out of choosing dumpy bridesmaids and harassed bridal party members at rehearsals if their shoes were the wrong colour or out of date. She had emergency shoes of all sizes in her closet, for last-minute replacements. It was not unusual for her to lend out her own jewellery.

I would like to believe that she barred me from events in order to shield me from stares, but we know our parents too well. I never could pull anything over my son, and my parents could not pull anything over me.

Besides, my mother was not wily enough to conceal her motives. She was secretive but not wily. Even her secrecy had more to do with shame than strategy. The most ordinary things embarrassed her: the commission she was getting, for example, or an error in computation. She lived in perpetual anxiety that curtain rods would come loose, drinks spill, centrepieces collapse.

In fact, it turns out that no one really stares, in the adult world. Children might be curious, but adults don't care one way or another. It's my stain, not theirs. Even if their initial reaction is surprise and confusion, they quickly overcome it. My mother lived in a child's world, a world in which she was still seven years old and hoping not to be scolded by teachers or mocked by classmates. She hadn't noticed that things changed as you grew older. And I imitated her. She failed to notice because she never grew up, and I failed to notice because I never looked up.

The therapist she took me to was blunt. 'Your mother has difficulty putting herself in other people's shoes,' he said.

'Maybe that's why she's always lending hers out,' I replied, and he laughed. He asked me to bring him a list, next time I came, of things I liked about myself and my goals in life. But I didn't go back. I didn't want to talk about myself or my goals.

I went to the Rate-MD website and looked up psychologists. Only one had unanimous raves: Peter Smith. A name that seems almost made up, like John Doe.

I phoned him. He sounded a little nervous on the phone, and very kind. He gave me an appointment for tomorrow—there had been a cancellation, he said.

I'm afraid of what he might say. I survived the counsellor, but she was herself bereaved. I don't think I would have been able to hear those things from anyone else. I would have told them to go to hell.

What can he do for me? Nothing—there's nothing anyone can do, unless they've found a way to bring the dead back to life. I won't even be able to speak about my son. Maybe I just want company—someone to connect to, without the pressure of having to give anything. Someone who won't mind that I'm a walking scarecrow, or made of tin. Ninety dollars for an hour of unencumbered company.

Though maybe he can also give me advice about finding a godparent for Pursie. It always seemed something to make fun of, when people left their fortune to their cats. And now I've become that person. I don't have a fortune, but whatever I have, I need to leave it for the care of Pursie.

As for letting Peter Smith know what has happened, I will write it down on a piece of paper and hand the paper to him. I am not able to say the words, *my son died*. I can only write them.

⸻

Peter sees people at his home. I suppose you can do that in a small town—make appointments with strangers seeking psychological help and trust them not to kill you. Maybe he can tell on the phone if someone's that far gone. Or maybe he runs some type of check.

He lives at the north end of town, on Shoemaker Crescent. Peter and the elves.

It's a suburban street, with the usual suburban houses, some of them quite large, but Peter's house is a bungalow, with two large windows to the left of the front door, and one window to the right, in a wall that must have once been a garage door. The only house on the street—and probably the entire neighbourhood—without a garage.

It was cramped inside. I gathered that Peter's wife and, if the bikes are anything to go by, two children, and either his father or his wife's father, who was sitting in the kitchen in an old bathrobe reading the newspaper, all live in five or six rooms and possibly a basement. We had to pass the old guy on the way to what Peter called the office—a small extension at the back of the kitchen.

Peter allowed me to choose one of two wicker chairs. He had first-meeting jitters, which I could see embarrassed him, but his nervousness dissolved the barriers between us, and I felt as if I'd known him a long time. On my left was a large window overlooking the garden, and I stared out at the bare shrubs and washed-out grass. If only there were another world behind the wardrobe or through the looking glass—

I handed him my note. He looked puzzled as he took it from my hand. The note said, *My eleven-year-old son was killed a week before school started. I don't want to talk about that.*

Peter nodded. I think he knew who I was before I came.

He said, 'This is your time, you can talk about anything at all. There aren't any rules here.' His voice caught and he wiped away a tear. I thought psychologists were supposed to be detached, but Peter didn't seem to mind giving way to his emotions.

It was contagious. I sat in his office and cried for an hour. I didn't look at him and I never did manage to say anything. When the hour was up he refused to take my cheque. 'I don't usually charge for a preliminary meeting,' he said. 'It's more of a tryout for clients.' Then he paused and said, 'I hope you come back.'

Mostly through sign language, at least on my part, we arranged another appointment. I see him again in three days.

What a nice man—and what an emaciated lump of uselessness I felt next to him!

Who was I before my son died? I can't even remember.

But I'm not sure I want to go back.

Peter with his children and family and little house on Shoemaker Crescent—how can he understand? What can he possibly say or do?

And what's the point, if his presence cuts through the trance produced by my venom-green pills? I need that trance.

At the same time, I don't want to hurt his feelings. I don't want him to think he's failed in some way.

'What do you say?' I asked Pursie. I rocked her in my arms, kissed her small head. 'Do you think Peter Smith will tell me my son blessed me with his death?' And to my amazement I began to laugh, had one of my fits. Laughed and laughed and couldn't stop.

The human brain, the things that go on in it— polarization, depolarization, channels closing and opening, chemicals travelling and being transformed and interacting in unimaginably complex ways—it's magic from start to finish. And here is my brain, malfunctioning, forgetting that my son is dead, and sparking one of my laughing fits, though it's more hysteria than mirth.

I'm back in movieland, as of yesterday. Went to the library and picked up forty DVDs.

Two hours, almost, with Peter Smith.

He waited for me to start, and when I didn't say anything, he asked, 'Is there someone in your life you feel you can trust?'

It was the perfect question, and it set me off on a long, nearly breathless tirade. First, my mother, and why I don't want to see her. It would be her drama, her tragedy. Then Neil, who let Sherry and her delinquent children destroy his life and his house, so that our son could not even visit, never mind sleep over. Next, my father's three marriages and all my half-brothers and half-sisters. And Fede who left me and Selena whom I can't find and Geri Wolfe, my former biology teacher, who moved to Greece.

He latched onto Ms. Wolfe, though I don't know why I even mentioned her. Maybe he chose her because she was the only one who wasn't either a disappointment or missing.

I explained about the unopened letters under the kitchen sink.

He understood exactly! 'I'd want to do the same thing,' he said. 'Most people say the most hurtful things, either intentionally or, probably more often, unintentionally. That's no excuse though. Anyhow, why should you have to put up with it?'

And he began telling me stories from his own life— another thing I thought psychologists weren't supposed to do. He told me about his mother's funeral, and the things people said. One woman got his mother's name wrong and said, looking at the open casket, 'Minerva looks more at peace now'—his mother's name was Malvina. He took it as a worse than tactless reference to the fact that his mother was an alcoholic. At the wake, someone asked for his mother's Janis Joplin records as a memento, and added that maybe the records were an omen. Another person made a joke about a prostitute at the gates of heaven. What took the cake, however, was a cousin who grabbed the opportunity to try to sell him life insurance, though to be fair, Peter said, he'd had a lot to drink by then.

I said, 'Maybe tragedy brings out cruelty in people. Maybe that's how they distance themselves. They're afraid of contamination.'

Peter nodded. 'Yes, it's possible. Even if it's not entirely conscious. Tragedy is frightening. It reminds us of the things we can't control.'

I said, 'Can I give you the letters? Maybe you could read them and, you know...'

'Act as filter? I'd be glad to.'

On the way out I caught a glimpse of myself in the hall mirror. I stared at my face, half white, half blotchy, like a two-sided Venetian mask. I had spent most of my life hating and hiding my face. How much of that had to do with my mother, and then Neil? I'd felt fine when I was with Fede, who never stopped telling me how sexy I was, and for whom every inch of my body was 'madness.' I felt fine with Neil too, during the first ten months. Why are we such reeds in the wind when it comes to others' perceptions of us?

I tried to imagine a mother who loved me. All the way home I tried to imagine it. I tried and I failed.

Yet through my son I remodelled my childhood, like a sculptor shaping stone or clay. I gave my son the love I wished I'd had, the childhood I'd fantasized for myself. To love someone is even better than being loved. My son loved me back, but that was a side benefit.

Now I'm left with a love that can perform no acts, reach no one. What good does it do, this paralytic love?

Love falls like veils, at random, from the sky. The veils fall here but not there, there but not here. And then they blow away.

Something Peter said, when I let him get a word in edgewise: I was describing my mother, and I concluded, 'I wasn't a good match for her.'

And he said, 'I'm trying to imagine the child who would be a good match for your mother. Maybe a child from Pluto?'

Pursie woke me with urgent meows.

I knew something was wrong—she almost never wakes

me, and the last time she meowed like that was when she'd had a mishap with duct tape. My son kept running into the sharp corner of his pine bed frame, especially at night, and finally in exasperation he'd taped a sponge to the edge. Pursie pulled at the end of the tape while my son was at school, and ended up with the strip stuck to her fur. I had no choice but to snip it off, leaving poor Pursie with a temporary crop circle on her back.

I wondered what trouble she'd got into this time. Maybe something had happened outside, in the new enclosure. I checked the clock: a quarter past six. Early for me, these days. Dragging myself out of bed, I followed Pursie to the living room.

She jumped on the windowsill and tried to say something. For one mad moment I thought the ghost of my son might be there, asking to come in. But what I saw instead when I came to the window was a different kind of spectral vision: there on the lawn, carefully arranged in a Celtic maze, were hundreds of stones, painted black.

I knew at once what this was about—Elias. In a blind rage I grabbed my sweater, pushed my bare feet into boots and ran outside. The black stones lay stark and sinister against the snow-coated grass. I began to kick them, and when that proved inadequate, I picked them up and threw them in the direction of the woods. I realized I was screaming—short, furious screams that punctuated each lifting and tossing. I had to tie the ends of my nightgown together so I wouldn't trip over it.

When the stones were all gone, I calmed down, more or less. Pursie must have seen Elias, my son's creepy friend, as he arranged the stones. Something made her identify him as an intruder, something made her want to alert me. Or maybe it's not that at all—maybe she was excited, seeing a friend of my son, whose absence is still an enigma to her.

It was always like that with Elias, wasn't it? Was he friend or foe, pathetic or scary, harmless or sneaky?

What has changed is that I don't have to feel torn now. I don't have to feel bad about this less than attractive side of myself. I admit freely that I am unable to care about Elias, who has lost his only friend and protector. I am filled with hostility, and even allow myself taboo thoughts about who lives and who dies.

My son had many friends, but Elias was the only one who ostensibly shared his interest in animal welfare. That was one reason my son befriended him, and I don't think the main one. The main one was that Elias was a breath away from being the class scapegoat, and my son believed it was his responsibility to keep Elias safe.

I told myself continually that Elias was a victim of his crazy upbringing, that he was only a child and needed kindness. I tried to be compassionate.

I did not succeed. His unpleasant demeanour and what I perceived as mental instability were disquieting, and though I tried to conceal my fears, I felt I had to be extra vigilant when he was around.

His parents belonged to a kooky cult that seemed to have only a handful of members. Elias was vegetarian, but not for the usual reasons—there was a long list of other food he wasn't permitted to eat. The restrictions, which seemed to change every day, were based on numerology, UFO sightings, lunar phases, and who knew what else. I was never sure whether the restrictions were also affected by what Elias did and didn't like.

The diet was only the tip of the iceberg. There were colour combinations he was not allowed to wear. Certain numbers and shapes were malign and had to be counterbalanced by amulets and incantations. Games, birthdays and holidays were all off limits. Elias could have easily broken the rules without his parents' knowledge, but he was too indoctrinated to disobey.

I no longer need to give Elias the benefit of my many doubts. Yes, poor, pale Elias, but I'm not sure he minds death and loss. For all I know, he's revelling in my son's death. He was always morbid, and I sometimes had a sense that he took a perverse pleasure in stories of suffering. He wrote an essay about suicide that was so disturbing I wanted to report it to social services, but I knew there was nothing they could do. Elias was housed, fed and schooled. We have freedom of worship in Canada, and that includes freedom to fuck up one's children.

My son was too young and generous to suspect Elias of wallowing in the dark side of life. He couldn't see that in Elias's confused world, what was good was bad, what was bad was good. The truth is that I thought Elias might harm my son in some way. It was irrational, but I couldn't overcome my self-centred attitude.

Well, I have been sufficiently punished. And now nothing more can happen to me. Let others worry about Elias. And let him keep his Celtic black-rock rituals to himself.

Remorse.

I am thinking of Elias, patiently painting those hundreds of stones, one by one, and bringing them here. Waking up before dawn, arranging them on the snowy ground, shivering in the cold. His way of dealing with my son's death.

He must have had help. Maybe the entire clan was here in the early hours of the morning. Maybe it was the sight of a dozen or more people slinking through the snow that unsettled Pursie.

My son would have wanted me to be nice to Elias. He was a better person than I have ever been or will be.

As for Elias, who knows what wonderful things he may accomplish, what good he may do in this world.

Sorry, Elias. I am not at my best.

My days slouch, like Yeats' rough beast, from Morning Retreats at the Bereavement Centre to meetings with Peter. Peter and I decided I'd see him twice a week. Again today I was there for nearly two hours—he waits for me to end the meeting, though he only charges for an hour. He told me as well that he's on a sliding scale. 'That's okay,' I said quickly, not wanting to elaborate on the irrelevance of what I spend my money on. I skirt around any topic related to my son's death. We covered that in the first meeting.

I also had a massage at the Bereavement Centre.

Fede and I used to give each other massages in front of Owen's oxymoronic, or simply moronic, stainless steel fireplace. 'Is it real fire?' I used to ask, which made Fede laugh.

I tried to give Neil a massage when we began our relationship, but he was bizarrely immune, and said he felt nothing, good or bad. As for giving me a massage, I assume he was trying to make a point or else ensure that he was not asked again. No one can be that incompetent—surely touching others is an instinct?

Marmie, who performed the healing touch on me, is also the massage therapist. She looks like someone who likes to dance—I can picture her in a Ginger Rogers outfit, breaking into a tap routine. Her pale orange, slightly comical afro is kept in place by a wide headband. I can't tell whether she's ten years older than me or ten years younger. She was wearing tight jeans and a white dress-blouse, or whatever it's called, with a bronze belt at her hips.

'Just make yourself comfortable,' she said, before leaving me in the small room. I removed all but my panties and lay down under the starched white sheet. I felt as if I'd entirely lost my bearings. I couldn't figure out what I was doing there, on that table, in that room.

Marmie fluttered back in. She was very talkative. 'Lots of knots,' she said as she settled her hands on my shoulders. 'All the stress, that's what does it.'

'You have an unusual name,' I said, veering away from anything to do with me. If only people understood what a precarious high-wire act these outings are for me—the slightest breeze or sneeze and I'll come crashing down. I want to carry a sign that says, 'Please talk about the weather.'

'You don't know the half of it,' Marmie said. 'My parents called me Marmalade, can you imagine? I was Marmalade and my twin sister was Meringue. Marmie and Merry for short. They were from South Africa—they had to escape when they fell in love. I guess they were so happy to be free, they lost their good sense.'

She went on to describe her summer in India.

She did a two-month dog-sitting house swap with a journalist from Jersey who lived with several dogs in a tiny seaside community near Chennai. What the journalist didn't tell her was that in June and July temperatures were deadly, hovering between thirty-eight and forty-four degrees from seven in the morning to ten at night. 'The fan will keep you cool,' she'd promised. She also forgot to mention that the shower and toilet were not in the house but down a walled passage in which a large nocturnal rat bounced about as soon as dusk fell. It did not occur to her to warn Marmie that a giant cobra resided at the waterhole, nor did she add that the screeching of children and mothers was ceaseless during the day, while nights brought a racket of religious chanting, howling dogs, sneering buffalo and clattering goats. Marmie found out only when she arrived that water had to be arduously pumped by hand, and that daily power cuts rendered the fridge all but useless and meant that even the fan, which in any case only recycled the heat, didn't work.

Despite this litany of hardship, Marmie's voice was low and soothing. I began to lose the thread as I drifted in and out of wakefulness, and only fragments of the conversation reached me: elephant temple, falling coconuts, fever ... In that Proustian half-sleep in which abstraction becomes tangible and takes on physical characteristics, I envisioned my life as two horizontal planes, one above the other, and the top one was a tractor that harrowed my pain down to the bottom plane and trapped it there. I was skimming on the top plane now, picturing the dogs, the power cuts, the geckos—

Marmie roused me by asking me to turn over.

She finished her story, and I felt sorry for her because

she'd been tricked. But that was my interpretation, not hers. She thought of the experience as an adventure and, remarkably, held no grudge at all against the swapper, and even threw a party for her when she came home. After all, she concluded cheerfully, everyone in the community suffered from these deprivations.

How different from me—always on the alert for injustice, as if I held the key to right and wrong. Neil and I had that in common, that obsession with injustice, or at least so it seemed.

That's what I talked to Peter about today: the two planes, and how Marmie didn't feel the swapper had pulled the wool over her eyes. I also told him about the overheard exchange between Neil and Dominic.

He said separating my present life into two planes showed enormous strength. Surfing on that top plane I had gone to the Bereavement Centre, I had gone for a massage, I had phoned him. I'd looked after Pursie and gone to the clinic for antibiotics when I was ill. I had built a fence and taken money out of the bank to pay for it. He said my strength staggered him. It staggered him that, all on my own and without the support of family and friends, I was able to do more than crawl on all fours, as I had that night when I ran out from my shower and begged my son to release me.

Marmie's swap sounded to him like something that had happened to his nephew. He told me a long story about a disastrous house swap in which the photo had been of another house! 'People do that all the time,' he said. 'It's classic. It doesn't take an obsession with injustice to wonder how someone could mislead another person that way.'

The conversation between Neil and Dominic shocked and upset him. I told him I'd started suspecting lately that Neil knew I was in the bedroom.

'That would be a very passive-aggressive way to communicate,' he said.

'Maybe allowing Sherry and her kids to move in was passive-aggressive, too,' I said.

'That's a big one. Usually when someone does something like that, there's a whole slew of reasons. None of them rational.'

'What really drives me crazy about her is that she calls herself a non-conformist. As if the way she lives is a lifestyle choice, and a superior one at that.'

'You know, Elise, if I had a dollar for every client who walked today into some therapist's office and used the word "non-conformist" as an excuse for being inconsiderate, for not doing things that would be helpful to themselves and others because it's a little unpleasant to do them, a bit of a strain, I'd be able to buy the state of Michigan.'

I half-smiled, but I was growing tired by then, and I took out my wallet and stood up. He looked tired as well.

'Thank you,' I said. 'Sorry about all the letters. I'll pay you for the extra time.'

He waved the topic away and showed me out. His father—I know now it's his father, not his father-in-law—was frying an omelette. He looked like a character in a Pinter play, dressed but with an old housecoat over his clothes and plaid slippers on his white, veiny feet. Fede would have wanted to photograph him.

I may have found Selena. There's a Selena Blanco on Facebook whose contacts include a Sebastian Blanco, and both are Canadian, though they live in B.C. and don't mention Toronto. I can't really see her face—the profile photo is of two people on skis, both wearing wool hats and viewed from a distance.

I'm afraid to contact her. Afraid of my jealousy, afraid of not being as kind to her as she was to me, afraid of having to tell her about my son.

Nevertheless, I sent her a message. It's so easy, with computers. A few words in a box, and then a small click to send them off into nowhereland.

I wrote:

> Hello, are you the Selena who lived in Toronto in 1981 with your mother and your brother Sebastian (who was a baby)? Do you remember being friends with a girl across the street named Elise?

And that was that.

Peter selected four letters from the bag of envelopes I gave him. They were there on the side table when I entered the room, like some voodoo talisman of unknown power. I was almost afraid to sit down.

Peter doesn't ask how I am when I arrive. He knows I don't want to answer that question, can't answer it. Instead he says, 'I'm glad to see you,' and lets me take it from there.

'Thanks for going through all that,' I said.

'Well, thank you for giving me your trust. I've taken the liberty—and of course it's very subjective, and only my very personal response—I've taken the liberty of selecting four letters I think might be acceptable. Most of the letters are run of the mill, so nothing lost if you bypass them. Mostly store-bought cards with only a signature and "thinking of you" or something along those lines. I've made a list of the senders, if you want to see it, but please don't feel you have to—there's nothing you have to do. Everything is up to you. Some letters are more personal but I wasn't sure about them. A few are from your son's friends, and one from the class as a whole. One boy, Elias—he sent a rather ... unusual letter.'

I told Peter about Elias and the black stones. I had the impression that he knew about the cult, though he didn't let on. 'I think my son felt sorry for him,' I said. 'But I just couldn't stand that kid. I didn't want him in our lives. I was torn between guilt and resentment. I still am.'

Peter nodded, and told me about a friend of his son—he has only one child, not two—who emptied the fridge and borrowed things without any intention of returning them. On the one hand, the kid had difficult circumstances to deal with, but on the other his behaviour was unacceptable.

'Our home is our one haven,' he said. 'It's the one place where we want to feel safe. We don't have to let anyone in who makes us uncomfortable in any way. We may be able to help these kids in other ways—or not—but I model limits and self-protection to my son. Elias was trespassing, period. You had, and have, every right to want to keep your distance from him.'

'Well, it's all irrelevant now,' I said.

'How you feel will always be relevant. Everyone has to earn the respect of others, and that includes children.'

As he spoke, I tentatively touched the envelopes on the table.

'Those four,' he said, 'I think, though I'm hesitant to decide for you, I think these are okay. I can't be sure, I'm not sure.'

I said, 'They'll be all right. You understand me.'

But I was only being polite, and it was with great trepidation that I unfolded the first letter. I was astounded to see that it was from Fede. Fede! How did he know where I was or what had happened to me?

I looked at the other return addresses: Geri Wolfe, Poppy and an aunt—my mother's sister.

In his tiny, neat handwriting, Fede had written:

> I saw your name in the paper, Elise. I
> was on the subway, and I think I cried
> out because people around me looked
> worried. I can't believe it—if you want
> me to kill that guy, please let me know,
> a life term in prison would be a small
> sacrifice for the pleasure. I've thought of
> you a million times over the years. I live
> in London (Ontario, that is) now, so not
> far at all. Divorced, two kids of whom
> I've got custody—I can't even imagine
> keeping my sanity if I lost them. I want
> to see you. I know there's nothing I can
> do, but I want at least to hold your hand
> uselessly. And do or not do whatever you
> want me to do or not do. I can take out
> the garbage, wash dishes, tidy up, bring
> you tea in bed—anything. If you don't
> hate me, that is. I deserve it if you hate
> me but I hope you can forgive me. Not
> that I expect you to be in a forgiving
> state of mind right now. I'm rambling
> like a fool and making a muddle of this
> but I seem to be good at that. With love
> and endless sorrow, Fede.

Poppy's letter was typed, but she'd used a calligraphy font and printed the text on ornate paper, with an embossed lilac border. She wrote:

> The world has lost a beautiful and
> rare child—brilliant, kind-hearted,
> exceptional in every way—and cannot
> be the same, ever. I am heartbroken
> beyond words. Cruel fate. I heard from
> your mother that you are not accepting
> visitors; I would do the same. For who
> can comprehend what you're going
> through? We are all feeling helpless and
> yet we want to help, but know those
> words will sound hollow. I treasure your
> weekend with us, long ago. Our arms
> are open.
>   Your loving sister, Poppy.

And from Geri, a card with a beautiful photograph of a cobbled walkway flanked by white stone walls and leading to a turquoise sea. Inside, she'd written:

> Dearest Elise,
>   Anne at Hawthorn told me what
> happened. I hope you will call me. I
> want to talk to you. I tried to find your
> phone number but no luck. I don't
> know if you know, but I lost two babies.

The first died of Sudden Infant Death
Syndrome. We decided to adopt, but the
child we were given turned out to have
a brain tumour and only survived a few
months. Grief can't be measured; but
if it could, nothing would come close
to losing a child. I want to invite you
to come to me here. I have a spacious
house facing the sea. You would have
your own room, your own time, and you
don't have to speak to a soul, not even
to me. I live on the western coast, just
south of Corfu. Please phone me if you
can at the number below, any time of
day or night. Or write. Or anything. My
heart breaks for you.

Your friend always, Geri.

That is as far as I got. I was crying too hard to look at
my aunt's letter. I wanted to go home, but I couldn't walk
through the kitchen sobbing, and I couldn't stop.

Peter brought me tea and four Fig Newtons on a plate.
How moving, those Fig Newtons—not very different
from the shoelaces and little cloth bag ... Sipping tea
and forcing food down my throat really did help, and I
managed to calm down.

I felt bad that I was being such a nuisance, and even
more so when Peter refused to let me drive home. He gave

me a long speech about his responsibilities, his assessment, his obligation to act on his assessment. I couldn't really take any of it in but I got the general drift—he didn't think I was up to driving and he wasn't going to take the chance. He was wrong, but I didn't argue.

Apologetically, and with the same jitters I'd witnessed at our first meeting, he removed various family items from his car and I climbed in.

As soon as I'd settled in the seat I felt engulfed by my solitude. I haven't been a passenger in years, and I was transported back to childhood treats: a drive with my grandparents, for example, to a farmer's market or a petting zoo. How I had treasured, on my son's behalf and mine, the sensation of family, plain and simple family, that my son had brought to my life—

It seems that everything good, from now on, will remind me of the good that is gone from my life. What miserly creatures we are! I wish suffering upon no one: I have always wanted the world to be a happy place. But I can no longer see joy and not sense, resentfully, my own exclusion from the maypole dance.

Peter promised to bring my car back later, when his wife came home. I fed Pursie and went straight to bed, and this morning, when I looked out the front window, I saw the old wreck, as we used to call it, parked in the driveway.

I'm still feeling bad that I put them to all that trouble. I will add something to my next cheque.

A very excited message from Selena. It will be harder
than ever now, telling her. She'll feel sick about her letter,
which is full of good cheer. I can't even reproduce it here.

She didn't say much about herself—only that she has
two daughters and is a single mom, but Sebastian shares a
duplex with her and acts as stand-in father and babysitter.
The Facebook photo is of her and Sebastian skiing. She's
beyond thrilled, hearing from me. It's like finding a long-
lost sister, she says, and she's flying over as soon as I send
her my address, and she was shrieking and hallooing all
day and why didn't I send a photo?

Now what?

february

Oh, I am livid! I've never been angrier—at least, not at my parents.

I reconnected my phone so I could call Selena—I didn't want to phone her from the mall. It's all right, though, because I have a new number, which no one knows. No one but Selena.

Selena told me that her mother killed herself a few months after the move to Alberta, by drinking antifreeze. Selena had phoned to tell me, and left a message with my mother.

'I never got the message!' I cried out.

'I'm not surprised,' she said. 'I asked the social worker to call, too. I had a dream that your parents would take us in. But your parents said no. It was asking a lot, you know, especially since Seb was only a baby.'

'Nothing would have made me happier—I'm sure I could have convinced them. I guess that's why they didn't tell me.'

Things went from bad to worse in the next few months. A fundamentalist aunt and uncle took them in. They neglected Sebastian and locked Selena in the closet for the smallest infraction.

Selena complained to the social workers, and the two of them were moved to the home of a childless Lithuanian couple who needed the foster-care payments. Everything in that place was top secret, Selena said. The couple spoke in hushed, cryptic tones, even when they were asking you to pass the salt. The foster father never revealed what he did for a living, and the foster mother was obsessed with her valuable figurine collection. Her other obsession was status. She lived in a fantasy world in which she was wealthy and highly respected, and she maintained that they were living in the tiny, low-rent apartment— only one step up from a crack house—temporarily, while their mansion was being repaired. It seems they really had had a large house, and had lost it, possibly because of a gambling problem. 'At least we could do what we wanted, providing we didn't touch her figurines.' Selena stayed home from school to look after her brother, and somehow no one noticed. 'That was a miracle,' she said.

There were two other peculiar homes after that, and finally, when she was fifteen and Sebastian six, a wonderful one in B.C., with a Unitarian minister and her husband. 'The nicest people in the world.'

But all that time they could have lived with us! We had three empty bedrooms—my parents could have at least told me Selena had phoned. They knew how much I missed her.

There's more, but I'm not up to writing it now. I'm still trying to digest the treachery and egoism of my parents.

I didn't tell Selena about my son. I didn't get a chance.

A long meeting with Peter about Selena. I could tell he was pleased that I'd reconnected the phone and contacted her. He has a very transparent face, though maybe it's because he doesn't try to hide anything.

He was disgusted by my parents' behaviour. He said it was like something out of a Shakespearean tragedy. Not delivering Selena's message, he said, was in the same category as locking a child in the closet. It just looked different.

My anger began to evaporate. I was sad for Selena and her brother, sad for myself, and sad even for my parents, who had refused to take in a sweet and wonderful girl like Selena and her orphaned baby brother. My father is gone, and as for my mother, she's lost her only grand-child, whom she loved as much as she is capable of loving anyone—in any case, more than she loved me.

I suppose it would have been scary for them: two strange children in the house, one of them a baby. Yet they had the means back then to hire help, and basic maintenance costs would have been covered by the government. They must have known how I felt about Selena. We were as close as sisters, and Selena was courteous and self-effacing. When she dined with us, she always hurried to clear the table and help with the dishes, as if it were understood that this was her job. My parents made a show of being concerned that I had no friends, and yet they deprived me of the one friend I did have. 'I don't really get it,' I said.

Peter shook his head dolefully. 'Betrayal by those closest to us is always the hardest to accept.'

I've been creating a library system for the Bereavement Centre. It wasn't anything I'd planned to do, but I mentioned the confusion in the book and video room to Marmie, and she said they've been waiting for someone with some computer knowledge to organize it all.

I volunteered for the task. I found a simple library program and I've been entering all the books, one by one. Books with titles like *Why Bad Things Happen to Good People* by Harold Kushner, good for him that he found an answer.

How is it that I can do this? I've gone into automatic. I do the things I myself have been programmed to do. I do them on the surfing plane, as Peter calls it. The entire time there is something tugging at my brain, whispering an anguished *no no no no no no*, but I go on.

I ran into Neil—literally. Neither of us was paying attention to our surroundings, and our carts collided at the supermarket. We both said 'Oh!' at the same time, when we saw each other.

I barely recognized him. He's grown a beard, and he's aged ten years or more. He'll be forty this year, but he looks like an old man. It hit me for the first time—I don't know why it was the first time—that he was going through the same thing I was. There is no difference at all. Yet there we were, at the supermarket, unable to say or do anything. Unable to fall to our knees and throw our arms around each other.

Instead I said, 'What are you doing here? I mean, in this supermarket.'

'I live around here,' he said hopelessly, and all my love for him came surging out of nowhere like some massive, blinding sandstorm.

'Where?'

'I rent a place on Reid.'

'Oh no, not Reid,' I groaned.

'Yeah, well,' he said, and switched abruptly to frozen anger. I'd have been frightened, but I know him.

I abandoned my cart and followed him as he shopped. Nothing could have kept me away. There was no decision or choice involved—it was magnetic gravitation.

He barely noticed what he was buying. Pasta, toilet

paper, light bulbs. I wasn't sure he knew I was there, but suddenly he said, 'Do you know what gets bloodstains off a wall?'

'Oh God, have you moved into a Hells Angels hideout?'

'No, it's my blood. I tripped over a cord and hit my head on the wall.'

'Oh no! Did you get it seen to?'

'No, it wasn't that bad. I just can't get the stain off.'

Nothing about Neil had ever been predictable. He'd eat without washing his hands no matter what state they were in, then discard a french fry that fell on the food court table. He had lived with Sherry in unspeakable conditions, and yet he wanted to get stains off a wall.

'I think the best thing is paint. I have some, I'll look after it. I had a fence built for Pursie,' I added, not knowing what I was saying, or why.

He began to sob, right there in the aisle. I didn't know what to do. He would not want to be touched. He never did want to be touched.

'I'll pay for this,' I said. 'You wait in the car. I'll be right there.'

He began to take out his wallet. 'Forget that,' I said.

He shuffled away, shoulders bent. His winter coat looked much too big for him, as if he were a child playing make-believe in his parents' clothes.

I used self-checkout, paid for his heartbreaking items, found his black Mazda. I reached out to scratch and stroke Ursula and Gudrun, who seemed more than usually happy to see me, then let myself into the passenger seat.

'You're coming?' he asked. He'd regained a degree of control.

'Yes.'

We drove in silence to Reid Court—a dismal, treeless street, its townhouses wrecked by several generations of partying students.

Neil's place was another casualty of student-loan living. It came furnished, if you could call it that, and Neil had brought almost nothing with him. The usual end-of-rental cleaners had been in, but they couldn't get rid of years of accumulated grime. 'Would you like something to drink?' Neil asked. 'I have vodka, tea, coffee, orange juice—no, I've run out of orange juice ...'

'I'll clean up the kitchen first. Why don't you go upstairs and rest?'

Neil was, as always, relieved to be excused.

I found large garbage bags and filled them with empty bottles and whatever else I could find to dispose of. It was impossible to eliminate the general atmosphere of delinquency and dilapidation, but I did what I could. The living room's french windows opened onto a small backyard, and I was able to drag the post-apocalyptic sofa, which reeked and was missing a cushion and two legs, out back. In that neighbourhood, it doesn't matter if you leave old furniture in the snow.

I've spent the last three days looking after Neil. He's been drinking and not eating and I think slowly poisoning himself with alcohol. He never drank much, but I guess he chose vodka over the venom-green pills.

I cleaned the house and painted over the bloodstain. I scrubbed the bathtub and made Neil soak in hot water and baking soda. I put away the alcohol and gave him my drugs instead. I threw out his blankets, which were covered with parakeet droppings, and bought new ones, along with bedsheets and towels. I shampooed and cut his hair.

'Why are you doing all this for me?' he asked. I had brought a steaming pot of spaghetti to the garage-sale kitchen table and was scooping out a large portion for him.

'You have half his DNA,' I said.

'I know you hate me,' he said. 'Even more now.'

I was taken aback. It seemed unlikely, somehow, that he was referring to Sherry and the kids. 'What do you mean, "now"?'

'It was my fault.'

'What are you talking about?'

'I was supposed to pick him up that morning, don't you remember? But Amy needed a lift to her Zumba class and back, and Sherry had the flu.'

'But our plans changed all the time. They were never really plans.'

'If I'd picked him up that morning the way I said I would,' Neil persisted. 'Or if we'd stayed married.'

'And if I'd called him in. Or pretended I hadn't overheard you. If the psychiatrist hadn't been on Demerol.'

'Yeah, I heard about that.'

'I never hated you for not picking him up,' I said. 'I don't even remember that. I'm angry about Amy and Karl and Sherry, but that's nothing new.'

'Well, I got my punishment.'

'I thought you were an atheist.'

'I didn't say God's punishment. I'm sorry, Elise. I'm sorry about everything.' He pushed his plate aside, and said, his voice trembling with emotion, 'I never minded how you look, you know. You were cute and sexy. I just used it as an excuse. I didn't want to get close. I didn't know how to be close until I was a father.'

I was too weary to be angry—angry that it took the death of our son for Neil to pay me a compliment, not to mention contribute a personal comment to the conversation. In the twelve years I'd known him, he had never given any indication that he liked a single thing about me. The topic of the connection between us was out of bounds.

'It doesn't matter now,' I said. 'Nothing does.'

'No, nothing does.'

There was a long silence as we each sank, alone and separate, into our own custom-designed purgatory.

Neil broke the silence. 'How do you do it?' he asked. 'How can you face the day?'

'I have to look after Pursie. I get through by taking the drugs I gave you. You can't go off them abruptly, by the way. Now you've started, you'll have to get a prescription.'

'What are they, exactly?' he asked.

I drew him a diagram of two neurons and the synaptic cleft between them, and showed him how receptors and neurotransmitters and reuptake operate. This was safe territory for Neil. What he liked more than anything was to talk about things unrelated to himself or anyone he knew. Politics, science, trivia—they calmed him, like the rocking motion of an infant's cradle. I felt it now, I felt him relax as he followed my explanations.

'That's the green pill,' I said. 'The sleeping pill is different. There's an ion channel here ...' I drew more diagrams, but when I began to explain action potential he stopped me.

'I can't concentrate,' he said. 'I can't concentrate on anything. I haven't been keeping up with my work, I don't know how I'll pay for everything.'

I found out, to my horror, that Sherry still had his credit card.

'Neil!' I shouted at him. 'I'm ordering you to cancel that card. Because Ursula and Gudrun need a home and food, even if you don't.'

I dialled the number, gave him the phone, and he cancelled Sherry's card. Music to my ears, I thought, even if it came too late. At least I'd never have to see or think of her again.

'You'll have to sell the house,' I said, when he described his situation.

'Where will she go?' he asked.

'Don't be crazy,' I pleaded. 'Hasn't she done enough harm to our little boy? For God's sake! She survived before you came along and she'll survive after you.'

I wanted to say, *She'll find some other sucker*, but I stopped myself just in time.

I've made an appointment with a lawyer.

I saw Ted Monroe, the lawyer. He's the one who handled the paperwork when we bought our houses, Neil and I. A young, charming, confident man, on top of the world, with framed studio photos of his young, happy family.

He said Sherry has no spousal rights at all, especially in view of all the money she's taken from Neil over the years.

I told him about the hoarding and the state of the house. 'I'm going to give her a week to vacate,' he said, as if it were his house. I didn't care what he charged—it was worth every penny, to have him take over. 'Whatever she leaves behind will be discarded.'

Then he said, 'I'm truly sorry about your son. Such a tragedy, so pointless. It makes me mad, you know? I have children, too. I know the judge who's hearing the case, by the way. If you want to make a victim impact statement, I'll be more than happy to help you pro bono. The guy's pleading guilty, from what I understand, unless there's some unexpected development. But I doubt there will be. He's signed a confession.'

'What's going to happen to him?' I asked.

'Well, it depends on the judge. If you make a victim impact statement, that has to be taken into consideration in the sentencing. He could get life.'

'Life!' I was shocked—I was imagining a suspended sentence or community service, or some form of house arrest.

'It's the maximum sentence for impaired driving leading to death, though the decision could include eligibility for parole in ten years. The judge could take into account that he owned up of his own accord, even though the lab results exonerated him. And he'll take other things into account: his record, his background, remorse. On the other hand, he was coming back from an AA meeting, which means he's been grappling with an addiction problem. That suggests a possible repeat—or not. It could go a lot of ways.'

I was hypnotized by Ted's legal reconstruction of my life. He was converting everything that had happened to me, creating a magic circle in which tragedy became disembodied and emotions thinned out. We could have been talking not about me and my son but about some theoretical case involving other people, strangers.

'I don't know,' I said. 'Nothing can bring my son back. It won't change anything, either way.'

'Can he be trusted not to cause more harm, if he gets away with it—that's the question,' Ted said.

'He wants to be forgiven,' I said. 'That's why he confessed.'

'Maybe. Well, think about it.' Ted leaned back in his chair and folded his arms. Forgiveness, the kind I meant, was outside his frame of reference, as he would have said. 'I think a victim statement is a good idea, personally. It's a tribute to your son, a chance to be heard by everyone. The media will be there. And I think if you don't do it, you'll regret it afterwards.'

'He has a nerve, wanting something from me, from *me!* Can you imagine?'

'Not really.'

'I don't want revenge.'

'Our legal system is based on justice, not revenge. Justice and protection. Anyhow the sentencing is not your responsibility, it's the judge's. Once all that is over, we can proceed to a civil suit. We can do that on a contingency basis—I'll only take a percentage of the settlement. People think that's not allowed in Ontario, but it is. But we can talk about that later. Why shouldn't he pay damages? I'm sure he can afford it. You can give the money to charity, if you like.'

He looked at his watch. He's a busy type of person, running from one thing to another. I thanked him and left. I almost wished I could stay inside the magic circle, but the hypnotic effect began to wear off as soon as I left the parking lot.

I'll see what Peter says.

Apparently Sherry's been calling Neil, crying on the phone, begging him to come back. She said she can't buy food for her children now that the card's been cancelled.

But Neil, I think for the first time in his life, stood up to her. He told her to apply for social assistance and use the food bank in the meantime, or hold a garage sale. He suggested Amy and Karl go to their father's.

All this Neil told me, not voluntarily, but in response to my questions. Neil always answers questions that are put to him—it's as if he feels that by living according to his principles, he ensures that he has no reason to lie. In any case, he's never been evasive with me when I asked for information.

Last night I began to worry about Sherry's children. What if their father was violent? They must have learned that belligerence from someone. Neil had no idea what the story was. All he knew about Chetwin was that he bought and sold Civil War antiques—muskets, shotguns, bayonets. It didn't sound too promising.

I decided to call him. It's easy, now that everyone has a website, to find people who run a business. Chetwin's site was professionally designed, but the antiques were mostly weapons.

Within five minutes of talking to Chetwin I felt ashamed of my suspicions. He turned out to be garrulous, affable, and even more unsure of himself than Neil. A Civil War antique hobby is apparently no different from stamp collecting.

He kept me on the phone for more than an hour. His complaints about his ex-wife were not exactly bitter—he's too laid-back for resentment. But he seemed to have an overwhelming need to unburden himself, as if he were still processing the experience. 'Don't be too hard on your ex,' he advised, though I hadn't said a word about Neil. 'Sherry's a genius at manipulation. She'd con the pants off Machiavelli—do you know who he was?'

Before I could answer, he enlightened me. 'Niccolo di Bernardo dei Machiavelli, 1469–1527. He's considered the master of political strategies. Even he doesn't hold a candle to Sherry. Don't blame your ex. Been there, done that. She puts on the pity-me face, she makes herself out to be helpless and pathetic. Don't believe a word of it. Every tear has a purpose.'

'How long were you married?' I asked.

'Eight years. Eight long years before I realized what I was up against and had enough. It's the kids I feel sorry for. You know what her first memory is? The first thing she remembers is going to all her neighbours pretending her dog died so they'd give her chocolate. It worked, too. Too bad it worked, huh? Too bad for me, and your ex, and you, and her sister, and our kids. I tried to hold on to them but I got a job on a tall ship up in Washington State, you know? I couldn't take them with me and by then I was so broke it isn't funny. But once her sister kicked her out, it didn't take her long to find your ex. Resourceful, that's Sherry. It's the only thing she'll get off her sorry ass for, finding someone to bleed.'

'She said her landlord kicked her out.'

He laughed. 'She said that? No, it was her sister. She's never paid rent in her life.'

'It's not her fault.' I suddenly and stupidly felt sorry for Sherry. 'Living in dirt and mess—it's an illness, I think.'

'You could say that about anybody, that they're ill. You could say it about Pol Pot, too. Listen, I used to come home—I was working at a garage back then—and I wouldn't be expecting much, you know? The kids looked after, a decent house, food. What did I get? Nothing. Nada. The kids were running around with filthy diapers and runny noses, eating M&Ms and chicken take-out for supper. They got scabies once, can you believe it? It was like living in the Third World. I told her off, but it didn't help. I tried to clean up but you may as well try to empty the ocean with a cup. She made out like she was really making an effort, but it was just an act. She'll say whatever it takes. I told you, she's a genius. She should get an Academy Award.'

'What will happen now? Can you take the kids?'

'Yeah, I guess. I'm still pretty broke, and I've got Madeleine and the baby so we had to get a bigger place ...

I don't suppose you'd be interested in any of my stuff? I have some great letters written by women to their soldier husbands, the spelling is a gas. Or a soldier's Bible, or a really great field trumpet, to decorate your windowsill. Everything's authenticated. I don't singe flags, if you know what I'm saying. I don't have anything to do with that sort of garbage. Oh, by the way, I'm really sorry about your son. I guess if it hadn't happened, I mean don't get me wrong, it's an awful thing, but Sherry would still be hanging on to your ex. It takes something like that to get rid of her. In my case it was rats and the city coming after us. I just couldn't take it anymore.'

I let him ramble on. I mostly tuned out, though at the end of the conversation I said I'd buy the letters and the Bible. He was very happy. Then he hesitated. 'Are you sure? I don't mean to be pushy.'

I discovered something. When he mentioned my son— it had nothing to do with me. It was as if I were watching television, or looking at a pizza flyer. The words didn't penetrate my world, they existed in an entirely different reality. It didn't matter what Chetwin said. I thought it would matter, but it didn't.

I've sent an email to Belinda, the real estate agent who sold us our houses when we first came to live here. She's a blue-eyed blonde with a cheerleader ponytail. I asked her to recommend a cleaning company that specializes in hard-to-clean properties, and told her I'd be ready for her to price the house on Cityview Drive in a week or so, when it was fixed up a bit. 'It's been through the wars,' I said.

I also contacted Donald, asked if he was available for some indoor renovations and painting for Neil. 'You'll need a powerful stripper to get the bird droppings off the floor,' I said, though, come to think of it, there wasn't that much exposed floor, when Sherry lived there. She'll be taking most of the bird shit with her.

Donald wrote back immediately and said he was free any time. I hope he won't be disappointed with a return to standard rates. I've seen Neil's accounts. He's nearly destitute.

All this running around and looking after things—I'm skidding, but at least I'm hanging on, more or less.

I've been going over to Neil's three times a day with food. I made him his favourite dessert, blueberry cheese-cake. He's given me a key, and doesn't mind if I go in and out freely, but I knock on the door before letting myself in. Sometimes he's out, walking the dogs, but most of the time he's asleep, and I wake him up to eat. I ate a slice of cheesecake with him, and for the first time since our son died, my body didn't respond to food with revulsion.

'I'm sorry for the way I told you,' I said, as I was leaving.

He didn't know what I was talking about. He doesn't remember the letter at all. He probably didn't read past the first sentence, just dashed out to the hospital. What a cold-hearted thing to do—leaving that letter on his doorstep!

'Was there a funeral?' I asked.

He stared at me in confusion. 'You'd know if there had been a funeral,' he finally said. His speech had changed to a drawl. I recognized the sensation that was slowing him down. Grief siphons your attention, distracts you, and you have to push through its cobwebs and thistles.

'I disconnected the phone,' I said. 'I haven't seen anyone, read anything. I wouldn't know if Martians had landed.'

Neil shook his head. 'They did two transplants. I asked not to know about it. I just signed whatever they gave me—they were in a mad rush, so no one bothered with me, which was what I wanted. He was cremated, the hospital looked after it. There's some letter somewhere ... I never picked up the remains.'

The word hung in the air, horrific, incomprehensible.

'I just couldn't find my way to the hospital. I kept going on Speedvale and I couldn't remember suddenly where Eramosa was. I got completely lost.'

'You never get lost.'

'I kept going round in circles. I don't even know how I finally ended up there.'

'Thank you for looking after everything. He wouldn't have wanted a funeral.' I leaned against the doorway, too weak to cry.

Neil didn't say anything, but he too seemed somehow to shrivel.

'We need to pick up the ashes,' I said, though I didn't really understand how I could stand there and talk about my son's remains. I must have been transformed into a marionette, I must have been uttering someone else's words.

'What for? It probably wouldn't even be him. Why would they bother?'

'We need to pick them up. We could scatter them in the forest as soon as the weather warms up. They won't throw them out, will they?'

'I don't think so, no.'

I asked him if he'd seen my mother. Neil emitted a characteristic snort, harsh and incredulous. 'She nearly drove me round the bend,' he said.

I didn't ask for details.

—

Peter is strongly in favour of a victim statement. I think he knows the child psychiatrist, at least by reputation, though I couldn't tell what he thinks of him.

'I agree,' he said, when I ranted about the audacity of my child's killer wanting something from me.

'I can't get over it. He wants me to forgive him so *he* can feel better! He wants to feel *better!* Guilt is unpleasant! Poor guy! I feel like throwing up, thinking about it.'

'Me too,' Peter said.

'And he stalked me for weeks—I didn't know it was him, but he parked in front of my house twice a week, for hours on end, waiting for me to come out.'

'Well, that's harassment and, I'd say, of questionable legality. Actually … I wasn't sure when to tell you. There was something from him, among those letters you gave me.'

I shuddered. At least it was not under my sink, defiling my house, defiling my son's death. I've only taken back the letters from Fede, Geri, Poppy and my aunt. The others, the ones Peter weeded through, are still with him.

'Well, what did he say?' I asked. I'm not afraid of my son's killer. His words can no more hurt me than the words on a billboard.

'Only that he wants to talk to you, has something important to tell you.'

'Why did he choose me? Why not Neil, for example?'

Peter said, 'I'll hazard a guess. I'll guess that he was scared of Neil.'

'All right, I'll write a statement. Not because I care about the sentencing one way or another—that's not my affair—but because my son can't speak. I will have to speak for him.'

More weeping. Me and Niobe. Will it never end?

Sherry's deadline for vacating was yesterday. This morning
I decided to drive out to Neil's: I wanted to satisfy myself
that she and her deviant offspring were really and truly
gone.

Neil's front lawn resembled a landfill. Halfway through
the loading, Sherry, as always, had given up and simply
left behind what she could not manage. Coat hangers,
pompoms, silver Christmas tree branches, and a thousand
other fossils from Sherry's life poked out of dented boxes
and mud-spattered plastic bags. As I forged a route to the
door, I saw that I was stepping on a file folder marked,
in bold handwriting, KARL'S ASTHMA AND VACCINATIONS.
Life, with its brutal organizational demands, was simply
too much for Sherry. Well, who was I to judge her for
floundering?

Inside, the house looked battered and smelled of birds
and rotten vegetables, but at least it was empty, apart
from a bed and two folding chairs. I'm sure Neil told
Sherry to take whatever she wanted.

I phoned a junk company. I described the situation, and
thought I'd heard wrong when they quoted their price,
but I asked them to come anyway. Half an hour later, a
white ten-wheeler drew up in front of the house and two
young men in overalls jumped out. They seemed to be in
a great hurry—maybe they were being paid by the load
rather than by the hour. They must have been friends, for

they had both mutilated their earlobes in the same way. The sight made me a little sick, and I had to look away.

It cost me a small fortune. The young men apologized for the thin layer of debris they were leaving behind— small, soggy bits that would take too long to clear. They wanted to make sure I didn't mind, they said, and that I wouldn't complain about them to their boss. They had it all down pat, those two.

I watched the white truck crawl away. In the end Sherry and her junk are just one more part of my son's world, vanishing forever.

I feel the thinnest of shells forming around me. If I were painting the shell on canvas, it would be a transparent membrane, like the membrane around a fetus, and it would have the faint imprint of Pursie and Marmie and Peter and maybe Selena and Sebastian, or Geri and Fede, or even Ted the lawyer and Donald the fence-builder. I don't know about Neil.

It's almost frightening, this shell. It's happening on its own, like some phenomenon of nature, like the moulting of a snake, for example, though in reverse.

Inside the shell, though, nothing has changed. My son's lifeless body has inhabited my own, is as much a part of me as my organs and limbs. I carry him wherever I go, the way I did when he was in my womb.

I remember how startled I was when Poppy asked me if I was jealous when my son ran into Neil's arms. She'd asked about Neil, and how that arrangement was working out, and I described how Neil bent down and opened his arms when our son, who was then four years old, came down the walk, and how our son hurried towards his embrace. 'And I guess you can't help feeling a wee bit jealous,' she said.

I looked at her, perplexed. A good thing for my son was a good thing for me—how could it be any other way?

I saw the world through my son's eyes. I still do. I can't break the habit. His vision, superimposed on mine, provides a simultaneous interpretation of what I see. I want to be my son.

So Neil has reverted to the pre-emptive freeze, the self-protective fuck-off. I always forget that part of Neil, even after a million and one encounters. I want to forget it. I want to believe it isn't real, or isn't serious, or isn't going to show up again. I take my Lunar Earth and Ultramarine Turquoise and dab at the slashes in the canvas. Compassion for Neil has been my downfall.

I say downfall because I have never been immune. I told myself I was immune, but I've never been immune, not from the day I pulled his crumpled-up sketches from the garbage pail at Mademoiselle Katyenka's.

How can he do this to me now—now, when I have

nothing, am nothing? If he can do it now, he has no soul, no heart.

I was putting away the dishes—his dishes. I said, 'The lawyer wants me to write a victim impact statement.'

You never know what will set Neil off. Those words were like a sorcerer's wand, instantly transforming Neil into someone, or something, else. With steely hostility and even loathing, he said, 'Oh, give the guy a break. He didn't intend to kill anyone. He took a painkiller, he fell asleep. I don't know why he went back to the police. I don't believe in putting people in cages and treating them as if they were subhuman.'

It wasn't what he said—it rarely is. It's the contempt in his voice, as if I've become in his eyes the personification of depravity.

When I wrote that the overheard conversation with Dominic did not come out of the blue, that's what I meant. We all have innumerable sides and moods, but Neil seemed possessed at times by an evil spirit, like Saul.

I said, imploring him, 'He killed our son. He knew what he was doing when he swallowed that pill. Why else did he confess?'

But Neil had withdrawn and would not talk to me. He bent down and cuddled Ursula, blocking me out. It was a familiar scene—Neil with his shield and spear. It was always unexpected and always familiar. I took my coat and left.

And still, and still, poor Neil!

———•———

Thinking about that exchange with Neil, I realized suddenly that the child psychiatrist may have wanted to leave it up to me. He might not have confessed formally had I not told Dr. Stuart, who must have contacted the police.

He had left it to me to decide whether I wanted to prosecute. He had placed that decision in my hands. Maybe it wasn't forgiveness he wanted. Maybe what he wanted was to hand me a weapon with which to fight back, in case I wanted to fight back.

And I took the weapon.

Imagine if Neil knew that part!

———•———

I told Peter, 'It's like he's two different people. One is gentle and caring.'

Peter said, 'If I had to pick between living with Jekyll and Hyde, or just Hyde, I'd choose Hyde any day. At least you'd know what to expect. I've worked with children in abusive situations, and the worst cases are those whose parents play good cop, bad cop. The kids lose all sense of the difference between pleasant and unpleasant. They might go through life not knowing one from the other.'

'Well, at least Neil was consistently loving towards our son.'

'You chose a good father for your child.'

'Yes. For all the difference it makes.'

He didn't answer. I knew, and he knew that I knew, that of course it made a difference, an enormous difference, during those eleven years. But this telescopic good has shrunk to something smaller than an atom, in the immensity of the darkness surrounding it.

'And he let Sherry deprive our son of a home.'

'Maybe he preferred to do things with his son after school. He sounds like the type of guy who prefers hanging out at Starbucks and the library to a domestic scene. He enjoyed taking your son to Canadian Tire to look for a new bike seat, and may not have thought anyone was missing out. You say he was never really attached to homey things.'

'Yes, it's true. He likes being with other people, as long as they're strangers. He likes being part of a crowd. Or liked. Now he's just in limbo.'

'When you think about it, Neil did keep your son away from Sherry and her kids. And he knew you were providing him with a normal home.'

'Yes. I was glad to have our son with me all the time. In Toronto I was lonely for our son when Neil took him, even though he lived down the street. I used to make up excuses to go over. Sudden need to read *Daisy Miller*. Sudden need to borrow batteries.'

'Neil was the one who was most affected by Sherry, I think.'

'I don't know what to do,' I said. 'Should I stop bringing food?'

'You know, you did exactly the right thing. The thing that seems to work best if you're dealing with a relative who's an alcoholic, for example, or a drifter. He needed you—he was sinking. He couldn't manage, and you reached out and took his hand. You helped, and then you exited.'

'So I shouldn't go back?'

'If you're worried, there's no harm peeking in on him. But I think he'll be okay, now that you've set him on course.'

'I've got Pursie, and he has Ursula and Gudrun ... The thing is, he was right about the psychiatrist. I don't believe in caging people up either.'

'The way I see it, at that moment Neil put the needs, so to speak, of the psychiatrist over yours. That's what stands out for me. Was that the time to climb on the soapbox and be sanctimonious? Or was it a time to listen to you and talk about the victim statement and how you feel about it? Was that the time to send you to Coventry or was it a time to support you?'

'Yes, he can be heartless.'

'Or his heart scares him so much, he locks it up. Sounds as if he's as hard on himself as he is on you. I'm thinking of the artwork he threw out, for one thing.'

'I wish he'd see you.'

'I'm not going anywhere. I'm here if he's ever ready.'

'I still love him.'

'We can love people but at the same time be completely exasperated by them, to the point where we can't even be with them.'

'He doesn't want my love, or anyone's love. I think he wanted our son's love, though.'

'Yes, I think he did.'

'There are so many horrible parents around. Why are we the ones to lose our child? And so many destructive people around—genocidal dictators, sadists—and our son, he was so caring, so interesting, he would have done such wonderful things. It isn't fair, you know? It isn't fair.'

march

Selena wants to come down here to see me. I told her, finally, that now was not the best time, and why.

I'm not up to the level of interaction a visit would bring—maybe I never will be. She's still a lovely person, a careful listener, and full of gratitude. But I have so little to offer in return.

It was my first time telling someone who didn't know. It was my first time saying the words, 'I had a son, he was killed in August.' My voice quivered and my throat contracted, but I said it.

I had to repeat the sentence three times—Selena couldn't hear me. Maybe it was the telephone line, but I think it's more likely that she couldn't take it in.

She said the right things. It turned out that she'd seen the headline when the child psychiatrist confessed. The story drew attention because the lab test was wrong, because of his profession, and because he confessed of his own accord, though the media doesn't know that he approached me first. No one knows, it seems, apart from Peter and Dr. Stuart.

But Selena hadn't read the story. It was too sad.

We reminisced. I reminded her of her butterfly-on-a-petal obsession and she said she still has one of the paintings I made for her. Her aunt—the one who locked her in the closet—threw out most of her things, but she'd managed to hold on to that one keepsake. She remembered things I've forgotten and I remembered things she's forgotten. Together we pieced together that happy year.

But I am no longer a normal person, and that past happiness began to oppress me. 'This is too painful,' I told her.

'Oh, I'm so sorry!' she gasped.

I'd upset her, and I felt bad about upsetting her. This was exactly what I'd wanted to avoid, could not avoid.

'There isn't any right or wrong thing you can do or say, Selena,' I told her.

'Please let me come down. I can stay in a motel, I just want to see you. Or you can come here, I can show you the coast and the mountains. Just the two of us.'

'I'm too crazy right now to do anything.'

'Yes, yes, I'm sorry,' she repeated. 'You know, all my life I aspired to be like you—so creative and smart and funny. From the day we met, that was what I wanted. So, in a way, I owe everything to you.'

'But you were the sane one. You had such a gift for sanity.'

'I guess we're never satisfied with who we are.'

'I don't even know who I am anymore,' I said. 'My identity was my son's mother. I'm a blank now. A complete blank.'

'I still love that blank,' she said.

I dreamt about Fede. There was no context for the dream: I had no age, no history. The two of us were having sex in a field of poppies and purple wildflowers, but we were doing it for Monet, who was working on a painting of us. His easel was set up a few feet away, among the flowers. And I was saying, 'These are Monet's secret paintings that no one knows about. Imagine what they'd fetch if they came to light.'

Everything's fallen apart again. I've cancelled Peter, I've cancelled Marmie.

It was a mistake to drive to Cityview Drive again, after Neil's deep freeze, but I wanted to see how the repairs were progressing. Or maybe I wanted something else, something to do with forgiveness, though I can't say whose.

Donald's truck was parked outside, next to Neil's Mazda.

I knocked on the front door, and when no one answered, I entered. A radio was blaring, and Donald, perched on a ladder, was plastering away. Neil had set himself up at the adjacent wall, the dogs at his feet. There was a six-pack on a stool and the relaxed atmosphere of male camaraderie.

Ursula and Gudrun came over to say hello, but Donald and Neil still hadn't noticed me. I knocked again so as not to startle them.

Donald turned and greeted me warmly, but Neil ignored me. He'd turned to stone, though only towards me—I could see he was getting on well with Donald. It came to me that Neil prefers the company of men because of the built-in distance of those interactions: emotional spheres, or even personal ones, are deliberately and effortlessly skirted. Why go there? It wouldn't occur to either of them.

My son was my ally. Not against Neil, whom I was careful to cast in the role of excellent friend, but against any disturbance at all, even when he didn't know it. I did not face the world alone, I faced it as my son's mother. It gave me such strength, such courage—

And now, here I was, on my own in this desolate house, half my face ablaze. Neil's onslaught all those years ago began pounding in my ears—*she turns my stomach, she turns my stomach.* For the first time since I heard those words, I felt unable to withstand the force of the attack.

I wrote a victim impact statement and sent it to Ted. There wasn't much to say in the end. I'm forty-one years old. I had one son. He loved animals. He persuaded his entire class to vow never to kill a spider or an ant. He was studying insects when he was killed. He wanted to help stop suffering and cruelty and speak for animals who cannot speak for themselves. He was brilliant in every way and loved by all who knew him. He received prizes at school and praise from all his teachers. He was creative and gentle and compassionate. He would have worked for justice. He's gone and my life does not seem worth living.

Peter sent an email. He said he was breaking all the rules by contacting me without my permission, but he was doing so partly as a member of the community.

> My wife and I would like to offer you our help
> if you want to attend the trial on Wednesday.
> We can pick you up, stay by your side, and
> give you whatever support you need. We
> make this offer as your neighbours. Or I can
> come on my own, if you'd rather be with
> someone you know a little better. Either way,

we are at your disposal. We can come late
and leave early, if you want to avoid crowds/
media. There may be a separate entrance—I
can check that for you.

It's a thoughtful gesture, and typical of Peter, and if
I wanted to go to the trial, the offer would have been
welcome. I've met Peter's wife and she's exactly what I
would have expected: warm, genuine, relaxed. She reads
Janet Evanovich—I saw a copy on the bathtub ledge.

But everything in me recoils at the thought of being
at the trial. My shell, if it was ever really there, has
disintegrated. I don't want to see the man who killed
my son, I don't want to witness strangers grinning and
gossiping about other things. And what if my mother
shows up?

The weeks of seeing Peter, cleaning for Neil, contacting
lawyers and real estate agents—it all seems a sort of aber-
ration. Something made it possible for me to do those
things, I don't know what. Whatever it was, it's gone.

I wasn't free to hate Neil when our son was alive, and
I'm not free to hate him now that our son is gone—he's
in too much pain.

But would hatred protect me from him? The only way
to escape Neil is to have nothing to do with him. Once
he sells the house, he will probably return to Toronto.
Maybe he'll have more children. He could easily find a
thirty-year-old partner. He's attractive, generous, and

smart, with a kind of dry humour that appeals to women. Maybe he'll have five children, and his loss will become nothing but a poignant and distant memory. The impulse that led him to search for Sherry may visit him again. He'll be more careful, I think, in future.

Exit Neil.

A dream about my son. A thrilling dream. He had acquired superpowers, and had made himself invisible. And that's all he was: invisible. And I'd been sad for nothing because he wasn't dead at all, I just couldn't see him. I was so happy, even though he hadn't figured out how to make himself visible again. I said, 'It's okay, it doesn't matter,' because we could still hear and touch him. And I began to think how we'd work things out at school—they'd have to mark the seat so that no one would sit on him by mistake—and how funny it would be when he rode his bike. I hugged him and kissed him and danced around the house.

In the transition from dream state to consciousness, when I was only half-awake, I still believed that my son was alive but invisible. I tried to cling to the dream. I thought, even if it's not true, I could pretend it is. It wasn't until I was drinking my coffee that the last remnant of dream logic faded.

If his spirit were here, would it be better than nothing,

or exactly the same as nothing? I don't want my son's spirit. I want to see him experience the world.

I want I want I want. My son and I used to joke about a neighbour we had for a year, a midlife-crisis man who was living up to all the clichés. He had left his family and bought a sports car, and he was looking for blonde models to date. He'd taken up mountain biking, too, and liked to parade around in his black and yellow Lycra shorts. One time, when we were both putting out the garbage, he told me he was going to the Aberfoyle farmer's market the next day. I didn't know about that market, and asked if we could follow him in our car. He panicked. He was afraid I'd socialize with him once we got there, and it would ruin his image. He wanted to strut around, playing the stud.

And I said to my son, 'He's reverted to age two. From morning to night, his mantra is *I want I want I want.* What a way to live!'

And my son said, 'It's his nervousness that's the problem. Pursie wants things, but she's not nervous about it.'

My wise son.

⸻

I'm thinking about calling Fede. It's five in the morning and Pursie is purring on my lap. The sleeping pills are not as effective as they once were, and even with the melatonin I can only count on seven hours now. That leaves seventeen more to tread through. Nor are shows and films providing the stupefaction they did only a month ago.

It's windy and wet outside, suffocating inside.

I don't think I can do this on my own anymore. I'd rather be hurt by inane comments and have the distraction and help that comes with them. What does it matter, what people say? It doesn't matter at all. I wanted to protect my son's memory, but that's not possible. I can only protect my own memory of him, and that memory can never be perforated or compromised or altered. No one can touch it. That memory is the shell.

I called him. We were on the phone for less than a minute. He's coming over tonight, after he's fed his kids—they're fifteen and seventeen but 'barely potty trained.' He'll phone as soon as he's on the road, so I'll know exactly when to expect him.

'Madness,' he said.

I wrote an email to my mother while I waited.

> I'm sorry I haven't been in touch until now. It was too hard for me to see anyone. I know this has been a terrible

time for you too. Let's get together
soon. If you want to come down here,
we could go out for a drive. Remember
Fede? He read about what happened and
he's coming over tonight. He's divorced
now, with two children. I've also found
Selena, my friend when I was ten. It's
okay that you didn't want to take her and
her brother in. You did what you could.
I had a nice letter from Poppy. I had a
letter from Geri Wolfe, too. She invited
me to visit her in Greece. Neil is selling
his house. Sherry's gone for good. He'll
probably move back to Toronto.
Love, Elise.

I've changed my mind. I called Fede at home to tell him
not to come, but he'd already left. I tried his cellphone.
There was no answer.

I can't see Fede, I can't see anyone. I want to stay in
bed, under the Coleman sleeping bag, with Pursie beside
me, for the rest of my life.

It was a form of denial, my venturing out into the
world. An attempt to be another person, someone who
can get through this. The drugs created that persona, but
I can't keep it up.

I'll have to leave a note for Fede. *Sorry you've come all this way, I am not up to a visit and have gone to sleep.*

I left the note for Fede on the front door, ran a bath, ate a bag of chips and went to bed. I took a sleeping pill, the melatonin, and two acetaminophen, and fell asleep with Pursie's paw in the palm of my hand. My sweet cat.

The phone rang this morning as I was drinking coffee on my son's bed. I didn't answer. It could only have been Selena or Fede, or a wrong number. I will have to disconnect the phone again, but I can't bear to talk to anyone today, even a faceless telephone worker.

Sudden panic: what if my mother comes down today? Why did I send her that email? I'll have to write again, put her off.

Three emails: from my mother, from Peter, from Neil. I couldn't figure out at first how Neil came to have my address, but then I remembered that he's been working with Donald.

I opened my mother's letter first. She wrote:

> Hi Elise. Good to hear from you. Yes,
> I want to come down, thank you for

allowing me. When is a good time? I'm
in the middle of an event so my days are
pretty booked up but I could manage
next Sunday afternoon. L, Mom.

When is a good time? Never. But I didn't say that. I
told her I'd let her know.

She's over the death of my son. But why should this
surprise me? She was always like that, my mother:
unwilling to be unhappy, and possessed of the most
remarkable powers of reinventing life to suit herself. She
shakes disagreeable things off like a wet puppy shaking
off water, and moves on.

Nothing in her letter about any of my news. I bore
her. She's always spoken to me as if I were a stranger she
happened to be sitting next to on the train, though at least
with a stranger she'd pretend to be interested.

Not to mention the subtle dig: *Thank you for allowing
me.* 'L,' I assume, stands for 'love.' Well, at least she got
to the first letter.

Peter on the other hand is concerned, hopes I'll book
another appointment, reminds me that he's on a sliding
scale. He can see me at my place if I prefer. I haven't
answered, but I will, later today.

I read Neil's email last. No greeting, of course—in
all the time I've known him, he's never once spoken my
name. He wrote:

I am moving to Toronto, staying with Dominic
till I find a place. The house sold for a good
price, thanks for arranging all that. Do you
need any money? Or anything else?

Impossible man.

I went out this morning to clean the bird bath and refill
the feeder. When we first moved here, we often went bird-
watching, my son and I, with our binoculars dangling
from our necks. We always took the same route, along
a five-kilometre trail of forest, fields, and little plank
bridges over streams. We became very involved with a
family of geese and tried to follow their peregrinations.
A young cyclist stopped by us one day and said, 'I saw
a merlin.' Then he rode off. I understood his excitement,
but my son was mystified and forever after would turn
to me at odd moments and say, comically, 'Mom, I saw a
merlin.' My son eventually outgrew these excursions, and
I'd been going on my own these past few summers, not
so much to watch birds as to meditate on the intricacies
of earth, water, trees, sky. I was sometimes lonely and
wished my son was with me, but those days were gone.
He was no longer my little boy.

It was cold out, and the wind slashed at me as I
changed the water in the feeder and emptied seeds onto

the tray. I didn't notice until I returned to the house that the note I'd left on the door had been replaced by one from Fede.

> Sorry honey but I was forced to be a
> peeping tom—I was worried. I looked
> in through the window, pretending
> to myself that I was the irresistibly
> handsome hero in a noir detective
> movie. I wasn't satisfied until I saw you
> take some drops at bedtime—vitamins? I
> figure anyone taking drops is still okay.
> So anyhow I called in sick and I'm
> still here, staying at an inordinately
> ugly motel (why are all motels so
> hideous?—it can't be cost-cutting alone,
> it must be part of some diabolical
> brainwashing scheme) and hoping,
> praying, desperately pleading with the
> gods that you'll let me see you. Sorry
> for inappropriate babbling, it's nerves.
> I'll be clinging to my cell all day, like a
> teenybopper. I bought you macaroons—
> you see, I do remember. Please call. I'll
> be waiting waiting waiting.

What should I do?

I'll let him in. What have I got to lose, really?

It's just that I have nothing to say, nothing to be. Well, he will see for himself, and he'll leave. He's expecting the old Elise. That person is gone forever.

Pursie went out to play in the enclosure. I followed her, and found myself opening the door to the shed and, almost involuntarily, stepping inside.

The painting I was working on when my son died was still on the easel, though exposure to the elements had warped the canvas. Looking at it now, I could hardly believe this sweet, light vision had once been mine—an old man asleep on a mattress, smiling at happy dreams.

I removed the canvas from the easel and turned it to face the wall. That painting was an act of betrayal, though to whom and what, I couldn't say. Or maybe it was the painting that had betrayed me. There comes a point when there are simply too many emotions, experienced too intensely, and the result is the murky grey-brown of the day's paints running down the drain. I was too muddled to think anymore, or even to feel.

I placed a blank canvas on the easel, and as if compelled or driven by an external force, as if I had no say at all, I twisted the caps off three tubes—red, grey, black. I had no plan, no vision—I barely knew what I was doing. I was shivering and my hands were numb with cold, but I found a brush. I mixed the colours, I moved my arm wildly along the canvas. I think I was moaning. I was painting the killing of my son, my child, my little boy.

I don't know how long I was there—at some point I must have switched on the heat. I was out of time, out of place, out of my mind. And then, finally, it was over. I realized I was sobbing, and also that Pursie was meowing at the shed door. I let her in, picked her up in my arms. She reached out to touch the canvas, then withdrew her paw quickly in surprise. I kissed her and muttered my love into her fur.

I wrote a few weeks ago that I would never be grateful again, and that hasn't changed. But there is a concept of *at least*. At least I have Pursie.

⁓

I phoned Fede at the motel.

'Elise! Elise! When can I come? What time is it? I'm starving, can I pick something up and bring it over? Don't worry, no dinosaur ears. I remember how much you dislike them.'

His voice hasn't changed at all, and since time has more or less collapsed for me, it made no difference that we hadn't spoken in years. 'Okay,' I said.

'See you very soon. Please don't change your mind. I'm

not sure I can take much more of this place, brought to you by Gropius' evil twin.'

'Just come in. The door's unlocked.'

'Oh. Okay. Sure.'

'Don't let my cat run out, though.'

'I won't.'

So Fede is on his way. And I'm glued to the sofa, laptop on my knees, with barely the strength to press the keys. The fit in the shed has sapped the marrow from my bones.

———

He knocked and walked in, pulled off his wet coat, pulled off his boots, and hurried over to the sofa. I'd forgotten his irrepressible energy, now an almost cartoonish contrast to my anaesthetised state.

He bent down and threw his arms around me, clasping me in a bear hug. I wasn't required to return the embrace— the awkward angle took care of that.

'Gorgeous as ever,' he said, studying me but not letting go. 'Only your eyes have changed. I'm going to burst into tears just looking at them.'

'Please help yourself to … whatever.' It was as if we were still students, picking up where we'd left off yesterday.

'Fucking cold. Fucking winter. I hate it. Oh well, nearly over now. I'll make some tea. I brought stuff from that store downtown—Stoned Store, I believe it's called.'

I wanted to smile, but my muscles refused to comply.

'Hello, kitty. What's your name?'

'Pursie,' I said. 'Short for Persephone.'

'My God, what a purr!'

He stroked Pursie, then went to the kitchen. I heard him fumbling behind me, putting on the kettle, taking things out of bags. I remembered how, when we were together, he'd sidle up against me while I puttered in Owen's kitchen, his body touching mine. I'd forgotten all about that, but it suddenly came back to me. Maybe 'sidle' is the wrong word. It was more of a feline motion. Casual but deliberate.

He returned to the sofa with two mugs of tea and a plate of macaroons. Everyone's giving me cookies ...

'No sugar, right?' he said, handing me my mug. He'd chosen one that said BILLIONS OF MEN—WHY ANIMAL TEST?

He's hardly changed in appearance. Some people change so radically that it's as if another actor is playing the older self in a film. Fede does look older—pouches under his eyes, grey threads in his hair—but he's the same Fede I knew all those years ago.

'I still have the portrait you made of me,' I said.

'Oh, Lordy, Lordy. I completely forgot about that!'

'You know, when my son died it all seemed so simple. I came home, I took a saw, I was going to saw the pipe from the furnace, go to sleep and never wake up. But I couldn't. I had to look after Pursie.'

Fede jumped up, ran to the bathroom, and shut the door. I heard him crying, though he was letting the water run. Finally he came out, wiping his face with a towel.

'Sorry,' he said. He slung the towel over his shoulder, and brought bits of food to the coffee table. Then he flopped down on the sofa, dipped a tortilla chip into hummus and said, 'I'll try to keep myself together. Have some food, you're looking too thin. Do you want a roll with butter? That used to be your favourite snack.'

'You haven't changed much in twenty years,' I said.

'Nineteen. You know, I obsessed about you for ages. But I figured that was it, you'd never forgive me for being such an arsehole.'

'Liar. So is that who you married, Kim Lee?'

'Kim—are you kidding? She could have anyone she wanted, why would she marry me? She married some huge lawyer, lives in a mansion in Rosedale. She even has a chauffeur. I wanted to call you when we broke up but I assumed you'd never want to talk to me again. I felt so bad about leaving the party with her. What kind of person does that?'

'You're wrong. I left first, don't you remember? I told you I had a headache and I took a taxi back to Owen's.'

'Really?'

'I saw the writing on the wall. You were pretty wasted, I'm not surprised you don't remember.'

'Yeah, the bad old days.'

'So who did you marry?' I asked him.

'It's a long story. I don't want to bore you.'

'If you weren't here I'd be watching *Foyle's War* and crying into my tea.'

He stretched out on the sofa, his feet on my lap, the container of hummus on his chest. He was the same old Fede. Well, why not? We have the genes we have, the brains we're born with.

He told me he'd married the niece of a big celebrity who'd won the Booker and several other international literary prizes. Three of this guy's books had been made into films, and one had received an Academy Award. Success hadn't turned his head, but it turned his niece's head. She became convinced that she too was a celebrity, and she aspired to ride on his coattails.

Fede met her before all this happened. She was ambitious, and Fede should have seen the signs, he said. But he didn't think she really took any of it seriously, because she laughed at herself for arranging her life in terms of what could advance her. They probably would have split up but she got pregnant, and Fede persuaded her to marry him. A year and half later they had another child—also unplanned.

Her uncle was now world-famous, and she herself had managed to land a few jobs in Canadian television. One show she'd worked on was picked up by NBC. She wasn't going to let life pass her by. She filed for divorce, handed Fede custody of their children, and went to live in Switzerland or London or New York or wherever her celebrity uncle happened to be. She eventually married a Hollywood scriptwriter and she's on a first-name basis with several megastars—Jennifer, Gwyneth, Forest ...

'She got what she wanted, I guess,' Fede sighed.

'But she sees her children?' I asked.

'She takes them to resorts in the summer, and sometimes drops by at Christmas. My mom and dad moved in, though, as soon as she left, and they've spoiled my kids rotten. I think my kids see their mother as a sort of bonus parent, more like a glamorous aunt.'

'And you didn't remarry?'

Fede shook his head. 'Too busy with work and the kids, too discouraged, didn't meet anyone—I don't know. A few short things here and there, nothing really.'

'What work do you do?'

'Airline publicity. Boring, though it pays well and I'm even unionized.' He paused and tried to hold my gaze, but I turned away. 'All we're doing is talking about me,' he said.

'I don't even want to *be* me, never mind talk about me. Show me some of the publicity stuff you do.'

'Sure. Do you have a computer?'

'Actually, I was wondering ...' It occurred to me that Fede would be the right person to open my son's laptop. I was afraid that if I didn't open it soon, what was there would vanish, and I wanted to see my son's last words, his last email. And everything else, too—his photos, his songs. Just not any sex sites he might have visited.

'Would you take a look at my son's laptop? It's just that there might be things on it he wouldn't want me to see. I want to read his last emails, but he'd be embarrassed if I saw a sex site. He was always moving the screen away from me so I wouldn't be able to see, or turning it off as soon as I came into his room.'

'Of course,' Fede said.

I removed his feet from my lap and went to fetch my son's silver laptop. The last frontier.

———

He set the laptop down on the coffee table, silver against black, and knelt before it.

'Are you sure it's okay that it's me?' he asked. 'Maybe it should be his dad?'

'I'll tell you about Neil later,' I said. 'He's the last person I'd ask.'

I was moved to see that Fede's hands trembled as he lifted the lid. 'No sex sites,' he said, after a few seconds. 'Or at least, nothing showing up, so if there were any, he's deleted them. I think it's safe for you to look.'

I hauled myself over to Fede's side of the table, sat beside him on the floor. My son hadn't logged out of his email, and his inbox stared out at me from the screen. My son's inbox! How many tortures are there in hell, exactly?

I moaned, and Fede put his arm around me. It helped to have Fede there, his arm bracing me. I would not have thought that anything could make a difference, but I was wrong.

When I was finally able to focus, I clicked on the 'Sent' folder. I wanted to read my son's last words. But his last sent email was the letter to CBS, about unfeeling references to animals on *The Big Bang*. I'd already seen that letter, when he asked me to look it over.

His last personal email was to Neil. The email read:

> hi dad this one is great too. But how will I fold
> it up like a pamphlet?

And Neil had replied:

> Here's the foldable version. Let me know if
> you're ok with the general idea. I'm sending it
> in pdf for now to make sure everything stays
> as is.

There were a few more emails from Neil, mostly links to funny videos—Snowball the Dancing Cockatoo, songs by Flight of the Conchords. I have no idea how I endured those emails. I felt like one of those computer images in which the pixels disintegrate. From human being to bits of sand.

'Who's Elias?' Fede asked. 'He sent a lot of emails.'

I didn't answer. Instead, I began opening those letters, and what I found there—it was hard to take in. Elias had sent my son to websites that displayed thousands of graphic photographs of hunted animals, factory animals, bombed animals, dogs beaten to death in China, elephants slaughtered in Africa ...

I ran to the toilet and vomited. I heard Fede's footsteps as he hurried after me.

It wasn't the images that made me feel so sick. It was the thought that my son had carried these images with him, and I had known nothing about it. I'd been right about ghoulish, morbid Elias after all. I should have trusted my instinct, I should have warned my son to stay away from him, even switched schools if necessary.

And the shock of not knowing this about my son—it left me reeling. I thought I was in touch with his world, but he'd taken a route I knew nothing about. He'd burdened himself with details about every atrocity Elias sent his way. And I'd failed to protect him.

Why hadn't I known? How had all this passed me by? How long had it been going on? My son had been secretive because he knew I'd disapprove. More than disapprove: I'd put an end to it.

I'd often lectured my son, when he didn't want to buy leather boots, for example, but was equally distressed by the pollution generated by synthetic products. I said, 'You can try to improve things but you can't be a purist, because everything you do is connected to some form of suffering, and if you drive yourself mad thinking about it, you'll end up not being useful to anyone. You have to compromise. You need *some* denial to survive.'

He didn't want to hear that lecture. He didn't want to compromise. He wanted to know. But knowing and collecting photographs are not the same thing. I would have explained that to him—I did explain it. I told him that obsessions always became self-serving. There has to be balance in life, and room for joy. There's exploitation and brutality everywhere—that's the sort of species we are, apparently. But we let the bad guys win if we become overwhelmed.

Had my son stopped making room for joy in the past year or two? Had I failed to notice? Had Neil known? Would Neil even think there was anything wrong with it—Neil, who was himself buried in chaos and passivity?

I remembered the discussion with Peter. It does make a difference, whether my son was happy. Even if nothing can bring him back, it makes a difference.

And in spite of all this, Pursie made me laugh. She was very interested in my vomiting and then in my vomit. She came over and put her paws on the toilet seat as I emptied the contents of my stomach. When I was through, she stretched her neck and sniffed inside. She seemed quite pleased with the outcome of her investigation.

Fede and I burst out laughing. 'I think she's got a puke fetish,' Fede said.

'Christ, she's got some on her.'

'Don't worry, sweetheart. She'll clean herself.'

And as if she'd understood our conversation, Pursie turned and calmly left the room.

I stripped and showered. I had bought a shower curtain decorated with hieroglyphics when we moved into the house, and my son had tried to decipher them. But the hieroglyphics turned out to be the designer's invention.

Fake hieroglyphics, I thought—a metaphor for every-thing. Water, at least, was simple. Hot water running down your neck, back, legs. It pushed away the past and the future. For a few seconds, it gave you the gift of nothing but the present.

Fede saw no reason to leave the bathroom. He leaned against the wall and said, 'Still the same Venus-on-a-shell body. Minus quite a few pounds. You've lost weight.'

We were never shy, Fede and I. We walked around like Adam and Eve in Owen's apartment. Adam and Eve before the fall. 'Remember that ugly fireplace?' I asked.

'I don't think the fireplace is what stands out in my memory.'

I stepped out of the shower, wrapped myself in a towel, and sat down on the edge of the tub. 'Well, that's it,' I said. 'I don't think anything more can happen.'

'Let's make a baby,' Fede said.

'What!?'

'I know it's crazy. I know you'll always be worrying—will it happen again? But you've decreased the odds, not increased them. Two freak accidents, what are the chances?'

'I'm too old,' I said.

'You're exactly the right age for a second child.'

'I can't start over, Fede,' I said. 'I'm too messed up.'

'Well, everyone's messed up. So what?'

'Are you saying live together?

'Of course live together—unless you don't want to.' He looked very dejected, suddenly, and I wondered how I'd failed to notice, back when I first knew him, how precarious his confidence was. Or maybe it had become precarious over the years.

'That's not it ... It's that you don't know me. I'm not the person I was.'

'I'll take any version I can get. It's time for my parents to stand on their own two feet anyhow. I don't think they're coping quite as well with the toilsome teens.'

'You're impulsive, Fede. You always were.'

'I know. But life is short.' He stopped, aghast at what

he'd said. 'I didn't—I'm sorry. What an insensitive thing to say.'

'No, you're right. Life *is* short, even when you live the usual amount of time. Or long, if you're waiting for it to end. Are you trying to be the knight in shining armour? That's not real life.'

'I promise to be difficult. I'm very neurotic, as you may remember. And my kids aren't exactly Flopsy and Mopsy.'

'You haven't even told me whether they're boys or girls.'

'One of each. Ian's seventeen, Sophie's nearly sixteen.'

'I don't really know what you're doing here, Fede. In my house, in my life. It doesn't make sense. But nothing makes sense anymore. I'm trapped in a nightmare, which means anything can happen. People I haven't seen in decades can suddenly show up and ask me to move in with them.'

'Am I making the nightmare worse, showing up like this?'

'No,' I said. 'Not worse. It's just that everything's disorienting, including you.'

'Yes, it all must seem very surreal to you.'

'I think the rest of my life will be surreal. What can ever make sense again, after this? Surreal, and sad.'

Fede didn't say anything, and for a few minutes we were silent. It was a tranquil silence, the kind that comes with trust. But my trust was that of a child who is too helpless and vulnerable to judge anyone or anything.

Yet when I finally spoke, I was aware of something

more than weary trust bolstering me up. Fede's generosity had always moved me. 'My poor son,' I said. 'He was weighed down, and I didn't know.'

Fede said, 'Well, it could just be a hormonal thing, you know. It's a very dramatic age—eleven, twelve. He would have found middle ground eventually.'

'If I'd known, I could have done something.'

'What?'

'I don't know.'

'We can't protect our kids from everything. Especially not from themselves.'

'I want to at least believe that he wasn't burdened.'

'Those photos don't tell the whole story. You would have known if he was depressed. He was probably just as good at blocking them out, or assimilating them, as we are.'

'I failed to create a perfect world for my son.'

'I wonder why,' Fede said.

'I can't do it,' I told him. 'I can't start over. I'm all emptied out.'

'Well, you can't just sit here and brood for the rest of your life.'

'I wouldn't survive another loss.'

'If you have another loss, I give you permission to get into a car with my mother.'

'I don't know if I could love another child,' I said.

'You wouldn't be able to help it. No one can, unless they're really fucked-up.'

'I feel a hundred years old.'

'Well, I feel sixteen years old, so between us we're okay.'

'Let me get dressed.'

'Of course. Sorry. I'll tidy up.'

When I came out of the bathroom in my T-shirt and jeans, Fede was standing at the counter with a bag of pretzels. 'These are the stalest pretzels I've ever, ever had,' he said. 'They're actually bendable.'

'My son's last email was a letter to CBS,' I said. The orange-red sleeping bag had slid to the floor, and I reached out for it, drew it over me on the sofa. 'And they won't even read it. Or if they do read it, they'll just laugh. And they'll make even meaner animal jokes, to show they don't care. At least he'll never know.'

'His last real email was to his dad, thanking him.'

'I might go to Greece.' I had no idea I was going to say those words.

'Greece?'

'My high-school teacher invited me.'

'Can't I come too? Pleeeese?'

'I was thinking of going soon,' I said, though I hadn't thought of it at all, until that moment. 'I can't stay here right now, I'll go mad—it's simply too painful. I'm just worried about Pursie. Do you think she'd be okay with a cat-sitter?'

'Of course. Cats are very flexible that way. As long as they're loved, they don't much care who's doing the loving. I could ask my sister. She adores cats.'

'I forgot you had a sister.'

'Two sisters. One is still in New Brunswick, married with four kids. They took over the store and made a success of it, believe it or not. That's Ginny. Marietta's got a partner too, Nora. They're in Toronto but always looking to get away.'

The thought of two strangers descending on Pursie made me uneasy. Were they quiet people? Would they be sensitive to Pursie's small, eccentric needs? Would she be bewildered and frightened? Every cat was different. Some liked change, but Pursie was so tuned in to me and to my son, to our habits and personalities, that I wasn't sure she'd adapt to anyone else. 'Maybe going away isn't a good idea,' I said.

'We could make it short, if you're anxious about Pursie. I have lots of vacation time accumulated. It can be our honeymoon. I get fantastic discounts, too. We could go first class. Now you can't say no—not with first class dangling before you.'

I looked at Fede, standing there with the bag of stale pretzels in his arms, at least four inches shorter than me, smiling his old playful smile, though it was slightly sadder now. His energy was exactly the same, though, and there was something tempting about it. I could lose myself a little in that energy. I could attach myself to his high spirits the way you attached yourself to a glider, and maybe it would help me—not to feel less pain, that was impossible—but to snub my pain, at least a little. But what was in it for Fede? In an abstract way, a theoretical way, I did love him. Seeing him leaning against the counter, hopefully, impishly, I recognized that I loved him. But it was not a love I could act upon. Why would he want someone so broken, so depleted?

'Why do you want me?' I asked. And I thought of my father, doubting that any man would desire me or love me or want to be with me.

'Who knows?' Fede shrugged, still grinning. I should have been affronted by his grin, but I knew him too well.

'My son will always be a barrier between us ... between me and anyone. Everyone.'

'I know, sweetheart,' he said. 'Come sit with us.'

Come sit with us—those words had been part of our private lovers' language. It was something Fede used to say, whether or not he was sitting, and it meant, 'Let's cuddle, because we do love each other, don't we?' I hadn't thought of that for nearly two decades. The phrase had vanished along with Fede.

It wasn't feasible, Fede's proposal. He wanted me to step into his life—a life that included two teenagers, another city, another house. He may as well have been asking me to run the country.

'What's your house like?' I asked.

'Big. Old. Needs new windows. Lots of trees on our street but two blocks away it's urban slum at its worst. But listen, I've been thinking for a while that it's time for a move. We could choose a new place together.'

A mountain of questions came tumbling at me. I felt exhausted. Yet it was this exhaustion that was swaying me in the direction of giving in, at least for the trip to Greece. How nice it would be to have someone look after luggage, rent a car, figure out where to go and how much to tip … But what a selfish consideration that was! The consideration of an invalid.

'What if I'd just be using you, Fede?'

'Oh, I love when you say my name. Hey, use me! I've always wanted to be a toy boy.'

I began to cry. 'I want my son back,' I sobbed. 'I want him to come with me to Greece.'

'I do too. You'll have to tell me everything there is to know about him. Or not—we can just think about him. Let's look at some dates,' he said. 'May I use your son's computer?'

'Fede,' I said, blowing my nose. 'I can see I'm going to have trouble getting rid of you.'

'That's right,' he said. 'Wild horses won't drag me away, this time.'

'I don't know,' I said, leaning my head back on the sofa. 'Maybe there aren't any answers. I'm so tired.'

I shut my eyes and saw my son. It was dark, where he was, like the inside of a tunnel, but the tunnel was as soft as a womb. There was a tall gate at the end, and my son pushed it open. He turned back and smiled at me.

And then he was gone.